Rm. 236

Bourji
Rm. 236

New Kid in Class

by
Anne Schraff

Perfection Learning Corporation
Logan, Iowa 51546–1099

Cover: Michael A. Aspengren

© 1997 by Perfection Learning® Corporation,
1000 North Second Avenue, P.O. Box 500
Logan, Iowa 51546–1099.
ISBN 0-7891-1968-4 Paperback
ISBN 0-7807-6641-5 Cover Craft®
All rights reserved. No part of this book may be
used or reproduced in any manner whatsoever
without written permission from the publisher.
Printed in the U.S.A.
  12 13 14 15 16 17 18 19 20 PP 08 07 06

NEW KID IN CLASS

1

SARAH JACKSON WAS daydreaming when Mrs. Blakely, the biology teacher, snapped out a question. "So what is the Second Law of Thermodynamics, Sarah?"

Sarah knew the answer. Besides being a science whiz, she had scored higher than any of her classmates on the SAT. She even had hopes of going to Harvard. But before Sarah could answer Mrs. Blakely's question, James Olson's hand shot up. James was new at Hawksville High School, and he was Sarah's lab partner. He seemed to know the answer to every question.

Sarah listened to James' deep, rich voice. "The Second Law of Thermodynamics: In any conversion of energy from one form to another, there is always a decrease in the amount of useful energy."

"Excellent," Mrs. Blakely cooed in admiration.

The teachers were all very taken with James. He'd just arrived from Jamaica last week and seemed to be an expert in everything. While the boys were shaking their heads and muttering things like "nerd," most of the girls were busy admiring the handsome boy's velvet brown skin and perfect features. He was tall and slender, with high cheekbones and eyes that glowed like golden-brown gems. Sarah found him very attractive. And she knew she was the envy of every girl in biology because he was her lab partner.

When class ended, Sarah met her best friend, Tina Cordell, in the hallway.

"What are you looking so dreamy about?" Tina asked.

"James Olson," Sarah sighed. "Isn't he amazing?"

"I guess," Tina said, shrugging her shoulders, "if you like that type."

Sarah frowned. "How can you say that?" she asked, heading for the fresh fruit machine. "He's so good-looking. And so smart." She pulled a huge orange from the vending machine and began peeling it.

NEW KID IN CLASS

"He's smart all right," Tina agreed. "In calculus, James corrected Mr. Massey, and he was right. But if you ask me—" Tina was suddenly interrupted by Sarah.

"Look, Tina!" Sarah whispered. "Here he comes!"

"Whoopee," said Tina, rolling her eyes.

"Hi, James," Sarah said, smiling her best. "Want part of my orange? I'll never be able to eat it all."

"No thanks," James said, his smile revealing perfect white teeth. "I carry my own vitamin C."

"Oh, that's right, you bring your lunch, don't you?" Sarah said. She'd noticed James never ate the cafeteria food.

"Yes, I've never cared much for school food," he answered.

"James, do you know Tina?" Sarah asked. "She's my best friend."

"Yes, she's in my calculus class. How are you?" James asked Tina politely.

"Reasonable," said Tina.

James frowned for a second as if puzzled by Tina's answer. Then he turned his attention back to Sarah. "Hey, Sarah, where's a good place to talk?"

Sarah looked at Tina, who rolled her eyes again and sighed. "Well, we could go out to the courtyard and sit under the trees," Sarah said, glancing at her watch. "I've got a few minutes 'til I have to get ready for track."

"Great," said James as he headed for the door to the courtyard.

"Be right with you, James," Sarah said. She turned to her friend. "Hey, Tina. Catch you later, okay?"

"Yeah, sure," Tina said, walking away.

Wonder what's wrong with her, Sarah thought as Tina left. Could she be jealous?

As Sarah exited the building, she noticed what a perfect spring day it was. The sun shone warmly from above, coaxing the flowering crab trees in the courtyard into bloom, and the birds chattered cheerfully as they scoured the floor of the courtyard for scraps.

James was sitting on a bench in a grassy spot under a tree. He looked up and smiled as Sarah approached.

"So, Sarah, tell me about yourself," James said. "Do you come from a big family?"

Sarah glanced at James. He had a wonderful smile, like a beam of sunlight.

"Well," she began, "I've got an older brother named Alex and a younger sister named Melissa. Melissa's kind of a brat, but Alex is pretty cool."

"So you're the middle child?" James said. "That's odd. So am I. It's a funny position to be in, isn't it? Too young to do what the older one does and too old to receive all the attention the younger one gets."

"Yeah," Sarah agreed, surprised at how mature James was compared to the other boys she knew.

"I'll bet you're the favorite child, though," James went on.

Sarah felt her face grow warm with embarrassment. She was both surprised and flattered that this handsome boy was showing such an interest in her.

"I think my parents try to treat us all the same," she said.

"Good for them," James said. "It's important that all of one's offspring develop a strong sense of self-esteem. But I see you have no problem with that. I can tell by the way you perform in class. You're very intelligent, aren't you?"

Sarah was embarrassed by the question. "I do all right," she shrugged.

"Don't be modest, Sarah," James said. "I've heard you're one of Hawksville's brightest."

Sarah quickly changed the subject. "James, you're from Jamaica, right?" James nodded. "So are you familiar with reggae?"

James chuckled. "Of course I'm familiar with reggae," he said. "Reggae is a popular Jamaican music developed in the 1960s. The root of reggae is American soul music. Reggae is characterized by its springy, off-beat rhythm, and many of its songs are political in nature."

"Wow! You sound like an encyclopedia," Sarah said.

"Well, it's hard to be from Jamaica and not know all about reggae," James explained.

"How about Bob Marley?" Sarah asked. "Do you like him? My brother has practically all of his CDs."

"Bob Marley—born in 1945, died in 1981. Sang with the Wailers. Love him,"

James said. "Who doesn't?"

Again Sarah was impressed. James was so smart!

Sarah checked the time. She hated to end their conversation, but she had to get to track practice.

"Sorry, James, but I have to go," she said, standing up.

"That's all right, Sarah. I need to get to the library, anyway. I'm going to read up on Shakespeare. We've begun studying him in British Literature. Quite an amazing fellow," James said. "See you later."

Well, if anyone can understand Shakespeare, Sarah thought, it's probably James.

When Sarah entered the building, Tina was waiting for her.

"Well, did he ask you out?" Tina asked.

"Of course not," Sarah replied. "We hardly know each other."

Tina watched as James disappeared down the hall. Then she said, "I don't know, Sarah. I think he's kind of weird. Besides, he smells funny—like an old man or something."

"Smells funny? Oh, Tina, don't be silly,"

Sarah said. Again she wondered if her friend were jealous of the attention James had given her.

"Well, he does—like some kind of spicy aftershave or something," Tina said, wrinkling her nose. "Besides, how can he be so smart and so mature?"

"He's from Jamaica, silly," Sarah said. "Maybe that's the way Jamaicans are."

"Maybe," Tina answered.

Sarah went to the locker room and changed for track practice. Her specialty was the mile. Just last week she'd come in second in the all-city relays.

"Hey, Sarah," Nate Bennett said as Sarah headed toward the athletic field. Nate was a tall, good-looking boy who was in trouble for his bad temper almost every week. Just yesterday he'd gotten into a fight with another student in physical education class. Sarah had heard that Mr. Brown, the PE teacher and track coach, had to break up the fight. Nate tried to claim that the other student had started it. But Coach Brown was familiar with Nate's temper and hauled him to the vice-principal's office. Then Mr. Potter gave Nate three days' detention to cool off.

"Hi, Nate," Sarah said coolly. Nate had asked Sarah for dates before, but she'd always turned him down. Lately he'd been dating Jenny Armstrong, a member of the track team. But Jenny had broken it off with him. She told Sarah he just wasn't her type.

"Hey, Sarah, you don't have to treat me like I'm a fly in your soup or something, you know," Nate said.

"Sorry, Nate, but I'm kind of busy," Sarah said.

"Big-time track star thinks she can just blow me off, huh?" Nate snapped. "Think you're pretty special nowadays, do you?"

"No, Nate, I don't," Sarah answered. "I'm just busy, that's all."

"Yeah, right," Nate scowled. "Everyone thinks they're such hot stuff around this school lately. It's like there's a big conspiracy going on to push Nate Bennett's face in the dirt."

Sarah could understand Nate's feelings. Between Jenny breaking up with him and Mr. Potter giving him detention, Nate probably did feel like the world was against him.

"Look, Nate," she said. "I heard about your getting detention. And I'm sorry you and Jenny broke up. But we all have bad things happen to us now and then. Now I've got to get to practice, okay? The coach is waiting."

"Yeah, you wouldn't want to disappoint Coach Brown," Nate said mockingly. "What a jerk." Obviously he was still angry at Mr. Brown for taking him to the vice-principal's office. Without saying good-bye, Nate turned around and sulked away.

What a loser, Sarah thought.

The girls did calisthenics and ran relays for about an hour. Just as they were preparing for the last race, Mr. Potter, the vice-principal, drove up in his station wagon. He got out of the car and opened the hatch to let out Sadie, his prize collie. Hooking a leash to her collar, Mr. Potter approached the track with the beautiful dog.

Sarah liked Mr. Potter. Some kids, like Nate Bennett, didn't, though. The vice-principal was in charge of discipline, so of course, students resented him for the punishments they received. But Sarah liked him. He often came to watch the athletes practice and was very supportive of the extracurricular programs at Hawksville High.

As Sarah readied herself for the next race, she noticed that someone else had come to watch. James Olson stood beside Mr. Potter. Immediately, Sarah dug her spikes into the dirt a little harder. She wanted to win this race.

"What a great-looking dog you've got there, Mr. Potter," Sarah heard James remark as she waited for the coach to give the signal.

Mr. Potter beamed. The Potters had no children, and they lavished all their attention on Sadie. "Yes, she's definitely the apple of our eye," he admitted.

James frowned. "I don't understand, sir," he said. "The apple of your eye? What does that mean?"

Mr. Potter laughed. "Sorry, James," he said. "I forgot you're not a native speaker of our language. What I meant to say was that we are very fond of her."

"Oh," James nodded, "now I understand. Thank you for explaining. You Americans have so many expressions." He stooped and held the dog's big head in his hands. "Look at those eyes. They're so expressive, almost perceptive."

Mr. Potter nodded his head. "Yes, Mrs. Potter swears that dog can actually understand our conversations."

"Amazing," James said.

Sarah had mixed feelings about the attention James was giving Sadie. She liked a guy who loved animals, but she didn't appreciate being upstaged by a dog.

Suddenly the whistle blew, and Sarah and the other runners were off. Sarah ran with all her strength around the track. Within a few seconds, she and Jenny Armstrong had taken the lead. Jenny was the best runner on the team. When Sarah had placed second last week in the all-city relays, Jenny had placed first. Now the two girls ran neck and neck for more than halfway around the track. But by the end of the race, Jenny pulled out ahead of Sarah by a nose and won.

Sarah was disappointed that she hadn't

impressed James by winning. But when she looked over at him, he was clapping his hands and gazing unmistakably at her. She instantly forgave him for his attention to Sadie.

"That was an impressive run," James said as Sarah came over. "You nearly beat her."

"Thanks," Sarah said. "One of these days I will, I hope. We've been competing against each other for years. Hi, Sadie," she said, crouching down to pet the collie. Sadie licked Sarah's face affectionately. "Hi, Mr. Potter."

"Hello, Sarah. Nice run," the vice-principal remarked.

Suddenly Sadie started to bark. Sarah turned her head and saw a cat in the yard across the street from the field. Sadie lunged away from Mr. Potter, pulling the leash out of his hand.

"Sadie!" Mr. Potter yelled. "Come back!"

Ignoring her owner's command, the big collie sprinted across the street, intent on chasing the cat.

"Sadie!" Sarah yelled. She looked at Mr. Potter. "How will you get her back?"

"Simple," said Mr. Potter. He reached into his pocket and pulled out what looked like a very small silver tube. Then he brought it to his lips and blew. To Sarah's surprise, no noise came out. But the dog immediately stopped in her tracks and trotted back to her master. Sarah was about to comment on this show of obedience to Mr. Potter when she noticed James. He had fallen to the ground and was covering his ears with his hands. His face was contorted in a painful grimace.

2

"JAMES," SARAH SAID, dropping on her knees beside him. "What's wrong?"

"My ears!" he moaned as he rolled back and forth in the grass. "That noise…"

"What noise? I didn't hear anything," Sarah said. She noticed that Coach Brown, some of the other runners, and even Nate Bennett had gathered around.

"You were able to hear this whistle, James?" Mr. Potter asked, obviously surprised.

"Yes," James groaned. He had stopped rolling around but was obviously still in pain. "What was it? It was excruciating."

"Just a dog whistle," said Mr. Potter. "It's supposed to be inaudible to human ears. I'm amazed you could hear it."

"My people are known for their keen sense of hearing," said James. He managed to sit up now, but he held the sides of his head as if it hurt to speak.

"Are you all right, James?" Sarah asked.

"Yes," James replied. "My head just hurts a little, but I'll be fine."

"I am so sorry, James," Mr. Potter said. "I never would have blown it had I known."

"It's all right, Mr. Potter," James said, getting to his feet.

Seeing that James was all right, the small crowd that had gathered started to break up. Coach Brown announced that practice was over.

"Well, I'd better get Sadie into the car," Mr. Potter said. "We have to stop at the grocery store. Are you sure you're all right, James?"

"Yes, sir, I'm fine," James said again. "Good-bye, Mr. Potter."

"Good-bye, James," Mr. Potter said, putting Sadie in the back of the wagon. "And good-bye, Sarah. Keep up the good work."

"Thanks, Mr. Potter. I will," Sarah replied.

"So do you walk home, Sarah?" James asked.

"Sometimes," Sarah answered, "but today I rode my bike. A lot of us runners do. It helps keeps us in shape for track. How about you?"

"I skate home," James said, nodding at the in-line skates on the ground beside him. "I just strap on my skates and away I go."

"Where do you live?" Sarah asked.

"Oh, about a mile south of here," James said.

Sarah frowned. "A mile south of here?" she repeated. "Isn't that the old warehouse district?"

"Yes," James replied. "It's not a very good neighborhood, but it's okay for now. In any case, it's only temporary." He quickly changed the subject. Sarah thought he was probably embarrassed to talk about his family's living conditions. "So, is that collie as intelligent as Mr. Potter says she is?" James asked.

"Yeah, she's a regular wonder dog," Sarah laughed.

"What a handsome specimen," James said. "I'll bet she's quite the show dog."

"Oh, she's won her share of ribbons, all right," Sarah said. She looked at James, once again noticing his handsome face and golden-brown eyes. She'd never seen eyes quite that color before. "Are you sure you're up to skating, James? You seemed to be in a lot of pain before."

"Don't worry, Sarah, I'm fine," he assured her, strapping on his skates. "Well, I've got to go. See you tomorrow." He waved and skated away toward the factory district.

After James had gone, Sarah noticed the smell of spice lingering in the air. It reminded her of her grandfather's aftershave lotion. Then she remembered what Tina had said about James smelling "funny." Must be his cologne or something, she thought. Could be some kind of herbal stuff from Jamaica. Oh well, if that's his only fault, I'm not going to worry about it.

As Sarah turned to head to the locker rooms, she spotted something shiny in the grass. Stooping down, she saw that it was a dog whistle. Mr. Potter must have dropped this, she said to herself, slipping it onto the chain she always wore around her neck. I'll give it back to him tomorrow, she thought.

Sarah approached the door to the gym and spotted Nate Bennett standing a few yards off, his hands shoved into his pockets. Despite his sullen appearance, Sarah was struck by his good looks. He wore his hair long, and it hung in shiny, dark curls down his neck. His eyes were a deep brown, and when he smiled, his face had a little-boy quality, somewhere between cute and handsome.

"Look, Nate," Sarah said. "I told you I'm busy. Will you leave me alone?"

"I only want to talk to you, Sarah," Nate said. "Just for a couple of minutes. That's all."

Even though Sarah didn't like Nate, she felt sorry for him. She'd heard he had a lousy home life. His mother had left the family when Nate was very small, and his father drank too much. As a result, Nate didn't receive much direction and was pretty much allowed to run the streets. Sarah knew that Nate was not the kind of guy she wanted to associate with.

"Sorry, Nate, I have to go," Sarah said.

Nate looked hard at Sarah. Then he said, "All right, go. But you're going to be sorry for treating me like a second-class citizen—you, Potter, Jenny—and all the rest of them. Even Coach Brown." He said "coach" in a mocking way.

Sarah had heard Nate's threats before. Every time a teacher had stood him in the corner in elementary school, Nate had threatened to get even. But for the most part, Sarah thought Nate was all talk. She ignored him and went into the building.

When Sarah got home, the aroma of her mom's homemade chili filled the apartment. Melissa was curled up on a couch reading a magazine, and Alex was beside her watching the news. He looked up when Sarah came into the room.

"Hey, Sarah, you look a little breathless," Alex said with a grin. "Is that from the bike ride, or do you have a new boyfriend?"

Sarah laughed. She'd never admit it, but she liked it when her brother teased her. "Well, there is this new guy," Sarah admitted. "He's from Jamaica and he's really special. I think he sort of likes me."

Alex kept grinning. "Jamaica, huh? That is exciting. What's he like? Is he a jock?"

NEW KID IN CLASS 21

"No, actually you'd probably think he's kind of nerdy," Sarah said. "He loves math and science and stuff."

Melissa had been watching the exchange between her brother and sister. Now she glared at Sarah. "How come you never talk to me about your boyfriends?" she demanded.

"Because you're ten years old, and you'd probably blab everything I told you to your dopey little friends," Sarah said.

"You really hate me, don't you?" Melissa said, sticking out her bottom lip.

"I don't hate you, you little twerp," Sarah said. It was true. Sarah didn't hate her little sister, but she sure found her irritating at times.

The phone rang and Sarah snatched it up, relieved to escape Melissa's whining. To Sarah's surprise, it was Mr. Potter.

"Sarah," Mr. Potter said, sounding upset, "something awful has happened! Sadie's been stolen!"

"Stolen?" Sarah asked. "Oh, Mr. Potter, what happened?"

"I took her to the grocery store right after I left the athletic field," the vice-principal began. "I left her in the car for a few minutes while I picked up a few things. When I came out, she was gone! I'm calling anyone who might have heard or seen anything."

"Gosh, I'm sorry, Mr. Potter, but this is the first I've heard about it," Sarah said. Suddenly a cold chill gripped her as she remembered the threatening remark Nate Bennett had made. But that's silly, she thought. Nate's all talk. And she hated to get him into any more trouble when she didn't know anything for sure.

"Well, we'll keep looking," Mr. Potter said in a disappointed voice. "If you remember anything at all, please let us know. We're worried sick."

"I will, Mr. Potter," Sarah promised. "I hope you get Sadie back real soon. She's such a wonderful dog." Sarah said goodbye and slowly put down the phone.

Suddenly James Olson came to mind. He'd been so impressed with the beautiful dog. Sarah could imagine how bad he'd feel when he found out what had happened. She wished she could talk to James, maybe even ask his advice on whether she should mention Nate's threat. But it was too soon to call him. They didn't know each other well enough yet. Still, Sarah was surprised to realize how quickly she was coming to care for James Olson and how often he was on her mind.

* * *

Thursday morning, Sarah met Mr. Potter coming into the school building.

"Mr. Potter, did—" Sarah began hopefully.

He shook his head sadly. "No sign of Sadie. We drove around and around the neighborhood. We must have talked to dozens of people. Nobody could help us. We put up signs, but we don't have much hope."

"She'll turn up, Mr. Potter," Sarah said. "Don't lose hope." She was so affected by the vice-principal's obvious distress that she forgot she was wearing the dog whistle.

Sarah headed down the hall to her locker. She saw James standing a few feet away, dialing his lock combination.

"Did you hear about Mr. Potter's dog?" Sarah asked, walking up to him.

"Yes, I did," James said. "It's too bad." He pulled his psychology book out of his locker and shook his head. "You just never know what's going to happen, do you?"

Sarah told him about Nate's threat. "Do you think I should tell Mr. Potter what Nate said?" she asked.

"If you really think he's involved," said James. "If not, no."

"I don't know," said Sarah. "Nate's had a couple of tough breaks lately. I'd hate to get him in trouble for something he didn't do."

"Suit yourself," said James. "But I'd say one thing is certain. More than likely, the Potters are never going to see Sadie again." Then he added, "I think the best thing they can do now is get a new puppy to get their minds off Sadie."

Sarah frowned. "You can't replace a dog like Sadie that easily," she said. When she was younger, she had owned a golden retriever named Rip. When Rip had died, she absolutely couldn't bring herself to get another pet.

"I wouldn't know," James said, closing his locker door. "I've never owned a pet."

"Never?" Sarah asked in surprise. They moved down the hall toward her locker. "Not even a gerbil or a parakeet?"

James shrugged. "Never wanted one. Animals are fascinating, but I'd much rather study them than keep them as pets." Sarah noticed that James had a faraway look in his eyes. "I remember some of the birds we had at home—tiny, bright purple creatures, no bigger than your thumb, with melodic voices…"

"I bet you're homesick, huh?" Sarah asked softly.

"I sure am," James admitted. "It seems like everything familiar is a million miles away."

Sarah felt a rush of pity for him. She tried to imagine what it would be like to be far away from everything she knew. She reached out impulsively and patted his hand. "It'll get better, James. We lived on a farm when I was little, and I had an awful time getting used to life in the city when we moved."

"Well, look at the lovebirds," Nate Bennett sneered. His locker was a few doors away from Sarah's, and he had come for his books to take to the detention center.

Sarah remembered Nate's threat from the night before. "Nate," she asked, "do you know anything about the disappearance of Mr. Potter's dog?"

"Me? Why are you blaming me?" Nate asked. "Why don't you suspect your new boyfriend here? Everybody's saying what a spooky dude he is. He's smarter than the teachers."

"Don't mind him, James," Sarah said. "He's a creep."

Nate looked at James. "Hey, aren't you from Bermuda or something?" he asked, slamming his locker.

"Jamaica," James replied.

"Same thing," Nate said. "Anyway, I hear they eat dogs down there, Sarah. Maybe that's what happened to Potter's dog. Maybe ol' James here had her for supper last night!"

"Nate, stop it!" Sarah cried, glaring at him. "Come on, James. Let's go."

As the two walked down the hall, Sarah said, "I'm sorry, James. That was a horrible thing for Nate to say."

James smiled calmly. "I don't let people like that bother me, Sarah. He was put here for a purpose, just like you and me. See you later." He waved as he turned into a classroom.

Put here for a purpose? That's an odd thing to say about someone like Nate Bennett, Sarah was thinking as she headed for history class. Lately it seemed Nate Bennett's only purpose was to annoy people.

In the classroom, she took her usual place behind Tina. Tina was reading a Stephen King book while she waited for class to begin.

"Hi, Tina," Sarah said.

"Hi," said Tina, looking up from her book.

"Did you hear about Mr. Potter's dog?" Sarah asked. Tina nodded. "I feel so bad for the Potters, losing her like that," Sarah added.

"I know," said Tina. "Who would do such a thing?"

Sarah lowered her voice. "Tina, last night after track practice Nate Bennett made a threat. He said we'd all be sorry here at school for treating him like dirt. Do you suppose he took the dog to get even with Mr. Potter for coming down so hard on him?"

"I wouldn't put it past him," Tina said. Then she changed the subject. "So how's the big romance with James going?"

Sarah heard the edge in her friend's voice. She really is jealous, Sarah thought. "There's no romance, Tina," she said. "We're just friends."

"Yeah, right," Tina said as the bell began to ring. "I still don't know about him, Sarah. He's a strange one."

Is she just saying that to keep me away from James? Sarah wondered.

The conversation came to an end when Miss Grimes, the history teacher, announced, "Today we'll be discussing the causes of World War I. Please prepare to take notes."

Sarah dug a pen and notebook out of her book bag and settled back in her chair. Miss Grimes turned on the overhead projector and began the discussion. Sarah put her elbow on her desk and rested her chin in her hand. Immediately James

Olson came to mind. Sarah realized that she detected the same spicy odor she had smelled the afternoon before. She put her hand to her nose. It's that cologne, she thought. I must have picked it up when I touched James' hand earlier. Sarah smiled and breathed in the smell again. While it was a little strong, it wasn't really unpleasant. And it made her think of James. She could hardly wait for biology class.

Seventh period, Sarah and James sat side by side at their lab table dissecting a frog. It was the last class of the day. Around the room, pairs of students huddled over their tables as well.

Sarah had never liked the smell of the biology lab, but today it seemed worse than normal. She wondered if it was the combination of the formaldehyde and James' strong cologne. "I hate lab," Sarah complained to James. "All these messy creatures, and the formaldehyde—it smells so bad." She didn't want to mention the cologne for fear of offending him.

"Well, you've got to be hands-on with science," James said, calmly studying the organs of the frog and jotting down notes in the lab report book. Sarah was glad he was doing the work today because the whole thing was making her queasy.

"Are you paying attention to our little friend here, Sarah?" James asked softly without looking up.

"Sorry," Sarah said. "I'm not big on animal intestines."

"Oh, but Sarah, when you get past the gore, look at the marvelous stretch of the muscles here," James said. "This is really an interesting specimen."

"You're a born scientist," Sarah commented.

James really warmed to the compliment. "Yes, I think I am. I've known I was going to be a scientist since I was very young. I'm always looking for the opportunity to locate interesting specimens and study them. That's what it's all about for a scientist, right?"

"I guess," Sarah said, glancing at the mangled frog on the table. Suddenly, the room began to move, and her legs felt weak. She knew she was going to be sick.

"Sarah, are you all right?" Mrs. Blakely asked, noticing how pale Sarah looked.

James glanced over at Sarah. "I think the frog and the smell of the formaldehyde are getting to her, Mrs. Blakely. May I take her outside for some air?"

"By all means, James," the teacher said.

James put his arm around Sarah's shoulders and led her out to the courtyard. Before they could reach a bench, Sarah felt her legs go out from under her. As James gently lowered her to the grass, she heard him say that he was going back into the building for some water.

Just before she blacked out completely, Sarah saw Nate Bennett standing over her. In his hands he held the bloody remains of a mouse. In numb terror, Sarah watched as the disgusting creature began to fall toward her. But before she could even think about screaming, she was overwhelmed by absolute, utter darkness.

3

SARAH COULD SMELL something spicy—cloves? cinnamon? She opened her eyes and realized she was still lying in the thick grass of the school courtyard. She lifted her head and saw James sitting next to her holding a paper cup. On the ground beside him was a crumpled paper towel. Even as Sarah watched, she saw red liquid seep through the paper towel. Sarah realized the towel was absorbing blood from whatever was wrapped in it.

"W-what is that?" Sarah gasped.

"A dead mouse," James said. "I found it on the ground next to you when I came back from getting this cup of water."

Sarah gasped again and struggled to sit up. Then she saw the blood splattered all over her white blouse. She felt the nausea return and put her hand to her mouth.

"Take it easy, Sarah," James said in his rich, soothing voice. "Just sit there a minute and breathe deeply. I'll get rid of this thing."

NEW KID IN CLASS 33

By the time James returned, Sarah was feeling a little better.

"I think...I think Nate Bennett dropped that mouse on me," she said.

"Nate Bennett?" James asked. Sarah nodded. "I should have known he'd do something like that. Probably took it from somebody's biology project. Are you all right now?"

"I'm fine," Sarah said, getting to her feet. "Just a little weak. How long have I been passed out?"

"Not long," James replied. "Just a couple of minutes. Do you think you can make it back to class?"

"I'll try," Sarah said. James put a hand under her elbow to steady her.

Mrs. Blakely met them at the door of the building. "There you are," the elderly teacher said. "I was just going to call the school nurse."

"We were just heading back to class, Mrs. Blakely," James said. "Sarah's fine now."

"I'm so glad to...Sarah, dear!" Mrs. Blakely exclaimed. "What on earth is on your blouse?"

"Just some blood, Mrs. Blakely," Sarah replied.

"Are you hurt?" Mrs. Blakely asked with concern.

"No, I'm fine," Sarah assured her. "It's a long story. I'm going home right after school to change."

"Well, come inside," Mrs. Blakely said. "You've only got a few minutes. The bell's about to ring."

Sarah was relieved. She didn't know if she could face any more frog guts that day.

When the bell rang, Sarah and James gathered their books and walked out the door together. As they headed toward their lockers, Sarah held her book bag in front of her to conceal the blood on her blouse.

"Sorry I fainted, James," she said. "I don't know what happened. I usually have a pretty strong stomach."

"It's all right, Sarah," James said. "I understand. You had quite a scare, what with Nate Bennett and everything. He's kind of a dangerous character, don't you think?"

NEW KID IN CLASS 35

Sarah nodded. "I never thought so before, but now I certainly do," she answered. "I guess I didn't realize just how resentful he is."

"Stay away from him, Sarah," James advised as they reached his locker. "People like that are a threat to everyone." He put the books he was carrying into his locker and took out his skates. Sarah noticed he never seemed to take any books home.

"Don't worry," Sarah said. "I don't plan on having any more to do with Nate Bennett than I have to. By the way, don't you ever have to study?"

"Once in a while," James said. "A lot of the stuff they're teaching here at Hawksville I already learned at my old school in Jamaica." He patted her on the shoulder. "I'll see you tomorrow, okay? I'm going back to biology for a while. I promised Mrs. Blakely I'd start work on a special project. Hey, I might need help at some point. Are you interested?"

"Sure," said Sarah, thrilled at the opportunity to work with James outside of school. Maybe this time she could show him how strong she really was. "Just let me know when."

"Do you have practice tonight?" James asked.

Sarah looked at her watch. "In about forty-five minutes."

"Maybe I'll stop by and watch you again," James said.

"Great," Sarah answered as James picked up his skates and headed back the way they'd come.

On her way to the bike rack, Sarah ran into Tina.

"You okay, Sarah?" Tina asked. "I saw James helping you out the door to the courtyard. I was in health class on second floor, and I can see the courtyard from where I sit."

"Yeah, I just sort of fainted," Sarah said.

"What happened?" Tina wanted to know.

"I'm not sure," Sarah answered. "I got sick in biology class. I guess it was the frogs and the formaldehyde. But you know what, Tina? While James was away getting me water, I think that creep Nate Bennett came by and threw a dead mouse on me. Look at the blood on my blouse."

"Gross!" Tina cried. "Wait a minute. Did you say Nate Bennett?"

"Yes, can you believe he'd do something so low?" Sarah replied.

"I don't know, Sarah," said Tina. "I never saw Nate Bennett in the courtyard. Of course, I couldn't watch every minute because Miss Davidson called on me. I think she saw me looking out the window. But if Nate Bennett was down there, he must have come and gone awfully quickly. Did you actually see him?"

Sarah hesitated. "Well, yeah," she said. "Right before I passed out. I'm sure it was him. Anyway, somebody threw a dead mouse on me. James said he found it when he got back from getting me a cup of water."

"James found it?" asked Tina. "Maybe he put that mouse on you just to make you all scared and clingy when you came to."

"Oh, Tina, that's ridiculous!" Sarah replied. "James would never do such a thing."

Tina shrugged. "All I know is, I never saw Nate Bennett down there. As far as I know, the only person who got near you was James Olson. I warned you about him, Sarah. There's something weird about him. Nobody's that perfect."

Sarah sighed. Would Tina never get over her jealousy? she wondered.

"Look, I've got to go," she said, wanting to end the conversation as quickly as possible. "I've got track practice in half an hour, but first I want to get home and soak this blouse in cold water."

"Wait, Sarah," Tina said. "Did you hear about Mr. Carlson's piranhas? They're gone. Somebody stole them right out of the tank."

Mr. Carlson was the other biology teacher at Hawksville. He had several aquariums around his lab.

"You're kidding!" Sarah cried. "Who would want those piranhas? They're dangerous."

"I don't know, but they're gone," Tina said. "And he's all upset."

"Gosh, first Mr. Potter's dog and then Mr. Carlson's fish. What next?" Sarah asked. "Wait a minute. Doesn't Nate Bennett have Mr. Carlson for biology?"

"Yeah, he's in my class," said Tina. "That is, when he's not in detention. And I think Mr. Carlson flunked him third quarter. Do you think Nate had something to do with it?"

"I don't know what to think," Sarah said. "Well, I've really got to run. I can't be late for track. See you later."

Sarah hurried home and put her blouse in the washing machine to soak. She was glad nobody was home yet so she wouldn't have to explain what happened. She'd be embarrassed to admit that she'd passed out while dissecting a frog. Alex would never let her live it down.

Sarah didn't feel like going to track practice today, but she knew she had to. She biked back to school and came onto the field about five minutes late.

"Jackson, you're late!" barked Coach Brown. He threw her a stern look.

"Sorry, Coach," Sarah replied. Sarah was sorry to anger Coach Brown. He was an excellent coach. He'd run track in college and had won a bronze medal in the

Olympics. She decided to run extra hard today, even though she didn't feel like it.

Sarah and the other girls practiced hard for about an hour. Then Coach Brown called a break while he went inside to take a phone call. Exhausted, Sarah crumpled onto the grass. She still hadn't quite recovered from the fainting incident that afternoon. When she looked up, she saw James Olson approaching.

Jenny Armstrong, who was sitting next to her, had seen James coming too. "That guy is so good-looking," Jenny said.

"Yeah," said Sarah, standing up and brushing the grass clippings from her legs. "Hi, James," she said, smiling. "Glad you could make it. We're just taking a little break."

"Hi, Sarah," said James. "Hi, Jenny. You're quite a runner."

"Thanks," answered Jenny. She opened her mouth to say more, but she was interrupted by the return of the coach.

"That's all for tonight, girls," Coach Brown said, smiling broadly. "Just found out my wife is in labor."

"That's wonderful, Mr. Brown," said

NEW KID IN CLASS 41

James. "Do you know if it's a boy or a girl?"

"Oh, it's a boy," said the coach proudly. "We know that from the ultrasound. Yep, after three precious little girls, I've finally got my boy.'"

"I bet he'll be a track star just like you, Coach," Jenny said, smiling.

"You bet he will," said Coach Brown. "My family is full of athletes. Hey, I've got to get right over to the hospital. See you tomorrow."

"Congratulations, Mr. Brown," said James. "That's great news."

Sarah was glad track practice was over, but she was sorry James hadn't gotten to see her run.

"Sorry, James," she said. "Maybe you can watch us practice tomorrow."

"Sure," James replied.

"Hey, James," Jenny said, still smiling her best. "Some of us are going to Raul's for tacos. Want to come?"

Raul's was a local restaurant where a lot of the high school kids hung out. It was known for its great Mexican food.

James looked at Sarah. "Are you going?" he asked.

"I suppose I could," Sarah answered. "I'm not busy, and Alex is watching Melissa 'til my parents get home." She turned to Jenny. "Is it okay with you, Jenny?"

For a fleeting second, Sarah thought she could see disappointment in Jenny's face. "Sure," Jenny said. "It's fine."

"I'll meet you at the bike rack in a few minutes, James," Sarah said. She and Jenny quickly headed for the locker room.

On the way, Jenny said, "Mind if I ask you something, Sarah?"

"No, go ahead," Sarah replied.

"Do you and James have a thing going?" Jenny asked.

Sarah looked at Jenny. The two girls had been friendly competitors for several years. But besides being the fastest runner on the track team, Jenny was also one of the prettiest girls at Hawksville High. And now it looked as if she might be interested in James. This was not good news.

"Well, not exactly," Sarah admitted reluctantly.

"He's so gorgeous," Jenny sighed. "Mind if I let him know I'm interested in him?"

Sarah shrugged and tried to act unconcerned. "I guess not," she said. I just hope he's not interested in you, she thought to herself.

"Great!" said Jenny. "Maybe I can get him alone at Raul's."

As Sarah showered, she noticed she still had the dog whistle around her neck. I've got to remember to get this back to Mr. Potter, she thought. I'll take it to him tomorrow.

Sarah dressed, grabbed her gear, and headed for the bike rack. She expected James to be waiting. In fact, she thought she detected the familiar odor of his cologne, but he was nowhere to be seen. As she scanned the school grounds, she heard a familiar voice.

"Hello, Sarah." It was Nate Bennett again. He was slouched against the building, hands stuffed in his pockets, as usual.

Sarah was shocked that he had the nerve to come near her after what he'd done earlier that day. "Nate Bennett, you make me sick!" she said. "I can't believe that little trick you pulled today!"

"What's the matter?" Nate sneered.

"Doesn't Miss Popularity like mice?"

"You're disgusting, Nate," Sarah said.

"Hey, I warned you, Sarah," Nate said. "Nobody gets away with treating Nate Bennett like dirt."

"So it was you behind the disappearance of Mr. Potter's dog," Sarah said. "And I suppose you stole Mr. Carlson's piranhas too."

Nate just raised his eyebrows and smiled.

"Well, I've had enough of you, Nate Bennett. I'm going straight to Mr. Potter tomorrow and tell him everything."

Nate seemed unconcerned. "Go ahead," he said, taking a few steps toward Sarah. "But you'll be wasting your time. You won't be able to prove a thing."

Suddenly Sarah remembered James' words about Nate: People like that are a threat to everyone. Sarah felt a cold finger of fear creep up her spine.

"Stay away from me, Nate Bennett," she said, getting on her bike. "I mean it. Stay away from me, or I'll go to the police."

Nate answered with a laugh. Then he turned and disappeared around the corner of the building.

A few seconds later, James showed up. Sarah was so relieved she could have kissed him.

"James, where have you been?" Sarah asked.

"Just skating around the track," James answered. "What's the matter, Sarah? You look upset."

"Nothing," Sarah said. "Let's just go to Raul's, okay? I need to relax for a while. Guess I'm still a little shaky from this afternoon."

"Sure," James said. "We'll go at a slow pace. There's no hurry, right?"

"Right," Sarah said, smiling. She was looking forward to being alone with James for the next few minutes.

Sarah rode her bike, and James skated next to her.

"Tell me about Jamaica, James," Sarah said, eager to get her mind off the events of the day.

"My homeland is beautiful," James said. "The climate is warm year-round, and every night the sky turns a deep lavender when the sun sets." He shook his head. "The moon against that lavender sky—

you've never seen anything like it!"

"I've never known a guy who looked at the moon before," Sarah said, obviously impressed. "Tell me more, James."

"We have mountains covered with lush vegetation—spectacular flowers like nothing you've ever seen and trees that grow over two hundred feet tall. And our jungles—oh, Sarah, you should see our jungles. They're overflowing with wondrous wildlife. I think that's how I first developed my love for science—by observing the creatures that came out of the jungle at night to drink at the stream near our village."

"What are your people like, James?" Sarah wanted to know.

"My people are wonderful—highly intelligent, logical, and creative. I think you'd like them, Sarah. You have a lot in common with them."

"I think I would too," Sarah said. "Oh, James, Jamaica sounds wonderful. I'd love to go there someday."

James raised his eyebrows and smiled. "Who knows?" he said. "Maybe you will."

Sarah was having such a nice conversation with James that she almost hated to reach Raul's. She knew that once inside, the other girls would be falling all over him—especially Jenny Armstrong.

"I love listening to you, James," Sarah said, getting off her bike and locking it to the rack next to the building. "I mean, you describe things in such a wonderful way."

"Well, I get carried away sometimes," James said. He slipped off his skates, tied the strings together, and hoisted them over his shoulder. "But I feel very strongly about the things I believe in. Shall we go in?" he asked, gallantly opening the door for her.

"Why not?" said Sarah, laughing.

Once inside, Sarah was relieved to see that the rest of the group hadn't shown up yet. The waitress seated them at a table in the corner. Sarah ordered a diet cola, but James didn't want anything.

"Did you ever go out for sports in Jamaica, James?" Sarah asked, eager to keep their conversation going for as long as possible.

"Not for team sports, no," James said. "But I hunted. That's considered a sport here, isn't it?"

"You mean you shoot animals?" Sarah asked, bothered by the idea that James might actually take an animal's life.

"No, no," James assured her. "I trap things. When you kill an animal, you're finished with it. But when you trap it alive, you can study it over time. There's the satisfaction," James said, nodding his head knowingly.

"Oh, so you catch an animal, study it, and then let it go again?" Sarah asked. "My brother used to catch frogs and keep them in a bucket, but he'd always let them go. Is that what you mean, James?"

"Something like that," James said, smiling.

Just then Jenny and some of the other track runners came into Raul's. Jenny came over to the booth where Sarah sat with James and said, "Hi, guys. I'm going up to order a soda. Be right back."

Sarah watched James closely. Few guys could resist Jenny, if only to take a long look at her. James was no exception. His gaze locked right on Jenny, and his eyes followed her as she walked to the counter.

"Pretty, isn't she?" Sarah said. She thought she might as well say it before he got embarrassed.

"Oh, yes, physically she's a beautiful specimen," James agreed. "How intelligent is she?"

"Oh, she does all right," Sarah said. "She's probably an average student. Why?"

"Just wondered," said James. "Most people I meet here are either very smart or very attractive." Then he smiled at Sarah. "But you're both."

Jenny came over to the booth carrying her soda. She sat next to Sarah, directly across from James.

"So, James," Jenny said, flashing him a charming smile, "I hear you're from Jamaica. How exciting."

"Yes, I am," James said. "But actually, I'm finding Hawksville pretty exciting." He looked directly at Sarah. Sarah noticed that Jenny was watching James.

Jenny tried again. "So, are you here permanently—I hope?"

"Probably not," said James. "My parents are here on a research grant for the Jamaican government. They're both scientists studying the environment. Once they're done here, more than likely we'll move on to another area to do the same thing."

This was the first time Sarah had heard that James' stay in Hawksville might only be temporary. Disappointment rushed through her.

"You're leaving?" she asked, trying not to sound the way she felt.

"Oh, not for a while, Sarah," James immediately assured her. He reached over and covered her hand with his.

Again, Sarah saw that Jenny was watching James closely.

"Well, I know when I'm beaten," said Jenny, standing up. "This is one competition I've definitely lost to you, Sarah." She smiled then and said, "But no hard feelings. At least you can't say I didn't try." Jenny picked up her soda and walked away.

Sarah was surprised that Jenny would give up on a boy so easily. She wasn't normally known to do so. Maybe it was because she and Sarah had been friends for so long. Sarah was also relieved that

NEW KID IN CLASS 51

Jenny wasn't angry about the whole thing. She didn't need two friends jealous of her.

"What was that all about?" James asked.

"Never mind," Sarah said, smiling. "You probably wouldn't understand. Ready to order?"

"You go ahead," said James. "I'm not hungry."

"Not hungry or thirsty? How do you stay alive?" Sarah joked. "I never see you eat or drink anything."

"I normally only eat one meal a day," James said. "That's all I require."

"Gosh, I wish I only required one meal a day," Sarah said, laughing. "I'd eat six if everything I ate didn't go straight to my hips."

"Nonsense," said James. "You have a perfect figure."

Sarah smiled. This guy was great.

4

BY THE TIME Sarah got home, it was almost dark. "Hi, Alex," she said to her brother, who was eating a large hoagie sandwich at the kitchen table. Sarah glanced around the room. "Where's Melissa?"

"Oh, she's around. Right now she's outside skating." Alex took a big bite of his sandwich.

Sarah frowned. "But it's almost dark. Shouldn't she be home by now?"

"I figure she'll come in when she's hungry," Alex said, wiping his mouth with a napkin. "She knows she's not allowed out after dark. Oh, by the way, Mom and Dad are going to be late. They went furniture shopping after work. We're supposed to make ourselves sandwiches."

"I've already eaten," Sarah said. "But I'll make Melissa a sandwich in a minute." First she wanted to check on her blouse. To her relief, all of the blood had come out. She put some soap in the washer and

NEW KID IN CLASS

started the delicate cycle. Then she went to the kitchen to make Melissa's sandwich.

Fifteen minutes later, Melissa still wasn't home. By now it was really dark. Worry nagged at Sarah. Nate Bennett lived in her neighborhood, and she hated to think of Melissa meeting up with him.

"We'd better go look for her," Sarah said.

"She's not a four-year-old, Sarah," Alex protested, "and this is a safe neighborhood. What are you getting so riled up about?"

"Because she's our responsibility when Mom and Dad aren't home," Sarah said, irritated by Alex's lack of concern. She didn't want to mention Nate Bennett. There was no point in getting Alex upset too.

"All right. If it'll make you happy, I'll go outside and give a yell," Alex said. "She's probably right around the corner."

"I'm going with you," Sarah said, heading out the door.

Once outside, they looked up and down the sidewalk. No Melissa.

"Melissa!" Alex shouted. Nothing. The neighborhood was quiet.

"Melissa!" Sarah shouted. "Where are you?"

Suddenly Melissa came into view, skating from around the corner, just as Alex had predicted. "For crying out loud," she said, "what are you yelling about?"

"Where have you been?" Sarah demanded, angry but relieved at the same time.

"Around the corner," Melissa said. "What's the big deal?"

"The big deal is you're supposed to be home by dark," Sarah said. "What were you so busy doing that you're late getting home?"

"Nothing," Melissa shrugged. "Just skating."

Sarah noticed that when Melissa spoke, she lowered her eyes, a sure sign that she was lying. Sarah and Alex glanced at each other knowingly.

"Melissa," Sarah said. "Tell the truth. What were you doing?"

"Just skating, that's all," Melissa insisted, still avoiding their eyes.

Alex said, "Look, Melissa, if you don't

NEW KID IN CLASS

tell the truth, we'll have to tell Mom and Dad that you were out after dark. You don't want that, do you?"

Melissa sighed loudly. "All right," she said. "If you have to know, I was talking to someone."

"Talking to someone?" Sarah asked. "Who?"

The ten-year-old tossed her head defiantly. "That's for me to know and you to find out. You never tell me anything, so why should I tell you? Besides, he made me promise not to tell."

"Melissa, Mom and Dad have told you a million times not to talk to strangers," Sarah said.

"He wasn't a stranger, stupid. He was from your school," Melissa said, sitting down on the porch step to take off her skates. Then she headed into the house, plopped down onto the couch, and folded her arms.

Sarah was growing impatient. She sat on the couch beside her sister. "Melissa, I want you to tell me who you talked to," she insisted.

"Melissa, I want you to tell me who you

talked to," Melissa repeated, mocking Sarah.

"You little twerp, you could have been in danger!" Sarah cried in exasperation.

"I wasn't in any danger, silly," Melissa said. "That boy has a crush on you, Sarah, which means he has oatmeal for brains. He just wanted a lock of your hair and a memento to put under his pillow at night!" Melissa laughed. "So I gave him a gob of hair off your hairbrush. It was really gross, but he didn't seem to mind. And remember that I.D. bracelet you threw away last week? Well, I dug it out of the trash and saved it. I gave him that too. You should have heard him. He was so-o-o-o happy, you would've thought I'd given him gold."

Alex had more influence over Melissa than Sarah did, so he came over and sat on the couch. "Look, Melissa. This isn't a game, do you hear me? Maybe this guy is dangerous. I want you to tell me who the guy was right now, okay?"

Melissa stopped smirking. "Honest? You think maybe he was a psycho or something?"

"Maybe. We won't know 'til you tell us who it was," Alex said.

"All right," Melissa said grudgingly. "I never saw him before, but he said he was Sarah's boyfriend. And he asked all kinds of stuff about Sarah, like what she eats and if she's healthy and stuff. He wanted to know practically everything about her."

"What did he say his name was?" Alex asked.

"Nate Bennett," Melissa said.

"Nate Bennett?" Sarah cried, her fears realized. "Oh, Alex, Nate Bennett is a troublemaker. Melissa should never have gone near him."

"Nate Bennett? Have I ever met him?" Alex asked, frowning.

"I don't think so," Sarah said. "He's kind of tall with dark eyes and long, curly hair."

Melissa nodded. "And he's handsome—I mean really handsome. He looks like one of those guys on the soaps. He smelled kind of funny, though."

"On the soaps?" Alex asked. "Melissa, you know Mom and Dad don't want you watching that stuff."

"Wait, Alex!" Sarah said. "Melissa, what do you mean he smelled funny?"

"He did," Melissa said. "Kind of spicy or something."

"But that sounds like James Olson, the new guy I told you about, Alex. He wears that weird cologne," Sarah said. "Are you sure it was Nate Bennett, Melissa?"

"That's what he said his name was," Melissa said. "And he looked just like you described him—long, curly hair and everything."

"Hmm," Sarah said. "Maybe Nate's wearing that stuff now too. Maybe it's the new rage or something. But why would Nate Bennett want some of my hair or my bracelet?"

"Sounds to me like he's just a love-struck guy who wants a couple of mementos from his girl. What's so bad about that?" Alex asked.

Sarah thought about it. Nate had asked her out in the past, but she had no idea he felt so strongly about her. If she weren't so angry at him, she might have been flattered.

"But I told you, he's a troublemaker," Sarah said. "Melissa, I don't want you ever talking to Nate Bennett, or anyone else you don't know, again."

"You're not going to tell Mom and Dad, are you?" Melissa asked. "I told you the truth."

"No, we won't tell them—this time," Alex said. "But if it ever happens again, they're going to know about it for sure, little sister."

Sarah wondered if she should tell her parents anyway. After all, there was a chance that Nate was dangerous. But Melissa didn't seem to be hurt. And things had been kind of stressed between the two girls lately. Maybe if she didn't tell Mom and Dad, she could patch up things with Melissa for awhile. Sarah decided to give it a try and keep quiet for now.

* * *

Sarah didn't see James until she was on her way to biology the next day. She told him about what had happened to Melissa, hoping he'd give her some advice on how to handle Nate Bennett.

James frowned. "What did Nate Bennett want with your little sister?"

"According to Melissa, he asked for a couple of keepsakes from me," Sarah said. "He told her he has a crush on me."

"What are you going to do?" James asked.

"I don't know, James," Sarah replied. "I was hoping you could give me some advice."

"Go to the police," James said. "I told you, that guy's dangerous."

"But what can they do to him? So far he's dropped a mouse on me and talked to my sister. I'm afraid I'd feel a little foolish talking to the police," Sarah said.

"Have you forgotten about his possible involvement in the disappearance of Mr. Potter's dog?" James asked. "And Mr. Carlson's piranhas? At least go to Mr. Potter. Maybe he can do something."

Mr. Potter! Sarah remembered that she still had his dog whistle.

"You're right," she told James. "I'll talk to Mr. Potter right after school." Suddenly a thought struck her. "James, how did you know Nate might be involved in the disappearance of Mr. Carlson's piranhas? I never told you that."

James hesitated and then said, "I just assumed it. I mean, it makes sense to me. Come on or we'll be late for class. I've got good news. Mrs. Blakely made me her lab assistant. She said she'd never seen anyone with such a talent for science."

"That's wonderful, James," Sarah said.

"Yes, she gave me a key to the lab and said I can continue working on that special project whenever I want." James stepped aside to allow Sarah to enter the lab first. "That's what I'm going to do today, and you're going to help me—sort of a lab assistant's assistant!"

Sarah smiled and asked, "But what about everyone else? What are they going to be doing?"

"After Mrs. Blakely takes attendance, she's taking the rest of the class to the auditorium to watch a movie. You and I get to work here alone today."

Sarah was thrilled. She finally got to work with James alone. "So, what's this project we're supposed to be doing?" Sarah asked.

"I'll show you as soon as the rest of

them leave," James said as they sat down at their lab table.

A few minutes later, Sarah and James were alone in the lab. James got up and dimmed the lights. "I've been working on a really exciting teaching device," he said. "And you're going to be the first one I try it out on—sort of my guinea pig, I guess you could say."

"Oh, boy, I'm flattered, James," Sarah laughed.

"Don't laugh," said James, taking something out of the supply closet. "You underestimate yourself, Sarah. I really respect your intelligence. I wouldn't ask somebody like Jenny Armstrong to help me with this. She's a striking example of beauty, but she just doesn't have the brain power you do. Okay, now, watch!" Sarah heard a click as if James had flipped some kind of switch.

"James!" Sarah gasped. Dozens of enormous scorpions crawled on the opposite wall. She shrank back in horrified disbelief.

"Stand still," James commanded. "Don't go near them. If a scorpion sees something moving, it will grasp it with its strong claws. If the prey tries to pull away, the scorpion stings the prey with great force, injecting venom into its victim."

"James—get rid of them!" Sarah screamed. She had never seen anything so hideous. "James, please!" she cried again. "Make them go away!"

Suddenly James flipped on the lights. As quickly as the scorpions had appeared, they were gone. In his hands, James held a device no larger than a ballpoint pen. "I projected them onto the wall, and you were fooled. That's marvelous," James said. "The experiment was a success!"

5

"JAMES, I WAS scared to death!" Sarah said, still shaken. "Why would you do such a thing to me?"

"In the name of science, Sarah. If I had tried the experiment on somebody else, say Jenny Armstrong, it wouldn't have proven anything. People with average intelligence are too easy to fool. But you have the highest I.Q. of any junior here at Hawksville. If you believed it, I knew the project was a success."

"James, how did you find out about my I.Q.?" Sarah asked. As far as she could remember, she'd never said anything to him.

"Oh, I accessed the school records through my computer at home," James said.

Sarah stared at him. "But why? Why did you do that?"

"Because I want to know everything about you," James replied. "And another thing—you scored higher than anyone else on the SAT."

"James," Sarah said with growing uneasiness, "I still don't get it. Why do you want to know all this stuff about me?"

"Because you're my partner," James said. "And we make a great team. There's no limit to what we could accomplish."

Sarah was hurt. She had begun to care deeply for James and had hoped he felt the same. Now she felt cheated. Was she only part of some scientific quest of his? Didn't she mean anything to him?

"James, I like science too, but I thought you and I…you know, were getting to be friends…or maybe more," Sarah said, trying to keep her voice from trembling.

"I'm sorry, Sarah," James said, "I'm not into dating. Science is too important to me at this time in my life." Maybe he didn't mean to be cruel when he said it, but tears filled Sarah's eyes. She felt embarrassed and humiliated.

"I don't think we should be lab partners anymore, James," she said with difficulty.

In a second, James was beside Sarah, his fingers clamping her wrist, holding her fast. "No, Sarah, don't say that," he insisted.

"We have to work together. We must! We still have so very much ground to cover."

"Let go of me, James," Sarah said. "That hurts."

James dropped her hand. "I'm sorry, Sarah, if I misled you. But you and I have to be lab partners. No one else is at my level, don't you see?"

"I don't think I'm at your level either, James," Sarah said. "I don't have the strong attraction for science that you do. I'm going to ask Mrs. Blakely to put me with someone else."

Just then, Mrs. Blakely returned with the rest of the class. James and Sarah sat in silence at their table for the last few minutes of the period. When the bell rang, James walked out the door without saying a word, and Sarah went up to Mrs. Blakely's desk.

"Mrs. Blakely, I need to talk to you," Sarah said.

"What is it, Sarah?" the teacher asked.

"It's about James, Mrs. Blakely," Sarah said. "I don't want to be lab partners with him anymore."

"What?" Mrs. Blakely asked in surprise.

NEW KID IN CLASS

"But why, Sarah? The two of you are my best students. I thought the partnership was an excellent match."

"I'd rather not talk about the reason, Mrs. Blakely," Sarah said. "Can you just put me with someone else? I don't care who. Anybody."

"I'd have to look at the class list again, Sarah," said the teacher. "I'll see what I can do." Suddenly she looked over Sarah's head and smiled. Sarah turned to see James Olson entering the room.

"Oh, James, you've come to work on your project?" Mrs. Blakely asked.

"Yes," said James, approaching the desk. "I'm so sorry, Mrs. Blakely. I hope Sarah isn't causing problems. She said she was going to ask for a new partner when I told her I wasn't interested in dating her."

Sarah was shocked. How could James share such private information with a teacher?

"That's what this is all about?" Mrs. Blakely asked. "Sarah, I'm surprised at you. I expected you of all people to realize that personal relationships shouldn't interfere where there's work to be done."

"But—" Sarah began.

"If I switched every student who was having a personal problem with his or her partner, biology class would turn into musical chairs." Mrs. Blakely chuckled and shook her head. "No, Sarah, try to work it out with James. Give it a couple of weeks. If there's still a problem, come see me then." She closed the briefcase that was on her desk and headed for the door. "Now, let's pretend this little conversation never took place, shall we?"

"Excellent idea," James agreed.

"You see, Sarah?" James said after Mrs. Blakely had gone. "We were meant to work together. Even Mrs. Blakely thinks so, and you can't argue with her, can you?"

Sarah looked at James' beautiful golden-brown eyes, and for the first time she saw an iciness there. She picked up her book bag and headed out the door, leaving James to work on his project alone.

There was no track practice that afternoon. According to the morning announcements, Coach Brown was still gone, and track practice would resume Monday.

NEW KID IN CLASS

On the way down the hall, Sarah met Jenny Armstrong. Jenny looked a little nervous.

"Um, Sarah," she said. "I don't want you to be mad at me or anything, but Jimmy asked me out just now. He…um, says you guys aren't dating."

"Jimmy?" Sarah asked blankly.

"James…James Olson," Jenny said. "He stopped me in the hall a few minutes ago and wanted to know if I would go out with him tonight."

"James asked you out?" Sarah asked. She was almost in shock.

"Yeah, I guess he was interested in me after all," Jenny answered. "Is that okay, Sarah? You and I have been friends for a long time, and I don't want anything to interfere with that."

"It's fine," Sarah said, still too surprised to react.

"Great," Jenny said. "See you at practice on Monday."

"Yeah, see you," said Sarah.

How could James ask Jenny out? Sarah wondered. He'd just told her he wasn't interested in dating. Sarah was even more hurt than before. James had obviously lied to her. He certainly was interested in dating—just not interested in dating her.

Sarah got her books from her locker and headed toward the exit, forgetting all about returning Mr. Potter's whistle. Suddenly she felt very much alone.

Lost in her thoughts, Sarah barely noticed the flurry of activity going on in the front office. Through the glass panels, she could see several teachers and Mr. Potter gathered around the principal. The teachers all looked very upset, and some were even in tears. Principal Grant was on the telephone, shaking her head and looking as if she were about to be ill.

Sarah opened the door to the office. "What's wrong?" she asked. "Has something happened?"

"It's Coach Brown's baby," Mr. Potter said gravely. "It's been stolen from the hospital!"

6

AN IMAGE OF Nate Bennett's face burst into Sarah's mind. Again she remembered his threat. "Even Coach Brown," Nate had said. Without realizing she was speaking aloud, Sarah said, "Oh, Nate, what have you done?"

"Nate?" Mr. Potter said. "Nate who?" Everyone in the room immediately turned to look at Sarah.

Mrs. Grant had hung up the phone just as Sarah spoke. "Do you know something about this, Sarah?" she demanded.

Sarah squirmed under their stares. "Well, I…um…" she stuttered.

"Sarah, come into my office, please," said the principal, leading the way down the office corridor. Sarah followed with Mr. Potter behind her.

Sarah was shaking. She'd never been in the principal's office before—for anything. Now she was being ordered in for questioning about a stolen baby. It wouldn't take them long to figure out that she'd had her suspicions about Nate Bennett all along—and hadn't reported them.

Mr. Potter closed the door, and the three of them sat down.

"Now, Sarah, if you have any information about the disappearance of Mr. Brown's baby, I want you to tell me—now!"

Sarah's heart was pounding. Mrs. Grant sounded angry, and Mr. Potter was staring hard at her. Once again the image of Nate Bennett came to mind. Despite her dislike of him, Sarah again felt a surge of sympathy. What if he didn't do it? She had no real proof. What if he had nothing to do with any of the disappearances? It wouldn't matter. Sarah knew that once she mentioned his name—Nate Bennett, the troublemaker, Nate Bennett, the juvenile delinquent—they'd go after him. And she'd be responsible.

"Sarah? We're waiting," said Mr. Potter.

Sarah took a deep breath and said, "I don't know anything."

"But out there you said…" Mr. Potter began.

NEW KID IN CLASS 73

"I was just mumbling," Sarah said. "I was just shocked by the news."

"You're sure you know nothing, Sarah?" Mrs. Grant asked.

Sarah shook her head. "No, I don't know who would take the coach's baby."

Mrs. Grant looked at Mr. Potter and raised her eyebrows as if to ask, "What do you think?"

"She's a good student," Mr. Potter said to the principal. "And very reliable."

Mrs. Grant was slow to speak. When she did, she looked directly at Sarah.

"Sarah, you're one of our finest students here at Hawksville," she began. "I've seen your records. As Mr. Potter said, you're intelligent and reliable. I know you can be depended on to do the right thing." The principal leaned forward in her chair. "And now we're depending on you, Sarah. If you know anything, *anything at all*, about the disappearance of Mr. Brown's baby, you need to tell us. Now."

"I don't know anything, Mrs. Grant," Sarah said.

A tense silence filled the room. Finally, Mrs. Grant said, "All right, Sarah. We have no reason not to believe you. You can go."

Sarah stood up and managed to say "Thank you" before walking out the door. She didn't know if she'd done the right thing or not. But she did know that she didn't feel right about accusing Nate Bennett.

* * *

Sarah was glad to get home that day. Her parents had taken the afternoon off and were just returning from playing golf when Sarah pulled her bike in the driveway. Alex was shooting baskets, and Melissa, as usual, was skating on the sidewalk in front of the house. Again Sarah thought of Nate Bennett's home life. No wonder he's like he is. How would I be if I didn't have such a great family? she wondered.

The conversation at dinner revolved around Mr. Brown's missing baby.

"Who would do such a thing?" Mrs. Jackson asked, shaking her head. "Those poor people must be worried sick."

"Do the police have any leads?" Mr. Jackson wanted to know. "I mean, did you hear anything at school today, Sarah?"

"No," Sarah said quickly. "I didn't hear about it until the end of the day." She decided not to mention her suspicions about Nate Bennett.

"Maybe the baby was abducted by aliens," Melissa suggested, humming the theme from *The Twilight Zone* and making her eyes round with mock fear.

"This is not funny, Melissa," Mrs. Jackson said sternly. "This is a human life we're talking about."

"Sorry, Mama," Melissa said.

"Remember the other day when Mr. Potter called and said his dog was missing?" Alex asked. "I wonder if the two events are connected?"

"I don't know how you'd connect the disappearance of a dog to the disappearance of a baby," Mr. Jackson said. "Who would have reason for wanting both?"

"It does seem far-fetched," Alex admitted. "But, Sarah, haven't there been some other disappearances at Hawksville High lately?"

"I guess somebody stole Mr. Carlson's piranhas," Sarah said. "But I don't know all the details. Anyone up for a movie tonight?" she asked, eager to change the subject.

"Not me," said Mrs. Jackson. "I think this afternoon of golf did me in." Mr. Jackson agreed.

"Sorry, got a date," Alex said. "But I'm surprised you're asking. I could have sworn I heard you raving about some new guy the other day. I thought maybe you'd be seeing him tonight."

"Things...um...didn't work out," Sarah said, avoiding her brother's eyes.

"I'd like to see a movie," said Melissa. "I'll go with you, Sarah."

Sarah smiled. Melissa wasn't too bad of a kid. The problem was just that—she was a kid. "Okay, you choose the movie," Sarah said. "We'll see what you want to see."

Melissa beamed with pleasure. "Thanks, Sarah," she said.

The girls went to see a comedy about a family who moves into a house that's haunted by the ghosts of the previous owners. Once they were seated, Melissa went to the concession stand to get a snack. While she was gone, Sarah glanced around the theater. Several rows ahead of her sat James and Jenny. James had his arm around Jenny, and Jenny was eating a box of popcorn. Sarah fumed and sank down into her seat. She certainly didn't want them to see her at the movies on a Friday night with her sister.

Sarah had a hard time concentrating on the movie. Not to disappoint Melissa, she tried to laugh at the funny parts, but she couldn't keep her gaze off James and Jenny. Occasionally she could hear James' deep, rich laugh or Jenny's giggle. They seemed to be having a wonderful time.

When the movie was over, Sarah hurried Melissa up the aisle and out the door of the theater.

"What's your hurry, Sarah?" Melissa asked. "Quit shoving."

"No hurry," Sarah answered once they were outside. "I just wanted to beat the crowd. Want to go for an ice cream?"

"Sure," said Melissa.

The two girls got home about 9:30. Mr. and Mrs. Jackson were in bed, and Alex was still on his date.

"Boy, Mom and Dad weren't kidding,"

Melissa said. "They really *were* tired. They must be getting old."

Sarah laughed. "They aren't getting old, silly," she said. "You're just so young—you never get tired."

"You can say that again," said Melissa. "Up for a board game?"

"No, thanks, Melissa," Sarah said. "I'm going to bed in a few minutes. I'm tired too."

"Thanks for taking me to the movie," Melissa said.

"No problem," Sarah replied. "You're not such a twerp after all," she teased.

"Gee, thanks," Melissa said, chuckling. "Good-night, Sarah."

"Good-night, Melissa." Sarah went to bed and immediately fell asleep. She was not aware of anything until she was awakened by the sound of the phone ringing at eight o'clock the next morning. A few seconds later, her mother tapped at her door.

"Sarah?" her mother called softly. "Are you awake?"

"Come on in, Mom," Sarah said. She yawned and sat up in bed as her mother

NEW KID IN CLASS

entered the room. Immediately Sarah saw that her mother looked worried.

"Sarah, Mrs. Armstrong is on the phone," Mrs. Jackson said. "Jenny didn't come home last night!"

"What?" Sarah cried.

"Mrs. Armstrong said Jenny was out with that Olson boy last night. When Mrs. Armstrong checked on her this morning, she wasn't there. Her bed hadn't been slept in! Mrs. Armstrong wants to know if you have any idea where Jenny might be."

"Did she talk to James?" Sarah asked hopefully.

"Yes, and he claims he dropped her off at her house around 10:30. Evidently they saw a movie and then went out for pizza."

"He's right, Mom," Sarah said. "I saw them at the theater last night."

Sarah felt sick as she remembered Nate's threat against Jenny. He must have intercepted her after James had dropped her off.

Sarah knew she had no choice now. She could no longer give Nate the benefit of the doubt. Everything that had happened lately, all the disappearances, involved people against whom Nate had a grudge.

Mr. Carlson had flunked Nate last quarter. Coach Brown had hauled Nate to the office, refusing to listen to Nate's claims that the other student had started the fight. Mr. Potter had given Nate three days' detention. And Jenny had broken up with Nate, claiming he wasn't good enough for her.

Now Sarah realized that it was probably only a matter of time before he got to her. Maybe he already had. Sarah still had no idea why he had approached Melissa the other night. Who knows what he was planning?

"Sarah, did you hear me? Mrs. Armstrong wants to know if you have any idea what might have happened to Jenny," Mrs. Jackson repeated.

"Yeah, I have an idea, Mom," Sarah said. "You'd better call the police."

7

A FEW MINUTES later, Mr. and Mrs. Armstrong were in the Jacksons' driveway. The police pulled in right behind them.

Sarah was trembling in spite of her efforts to keep calm. She told her story to the two police officers, about Nate's threats and the grudges he had against all of the unfortunate people involved.

Mrs. Armstrong cried softly on the couch, and Mr. Armstrong looked physically ill.

After the officer asked Sarah a few more questions, Mr. Jackson asked, "What will you do now?"

"First thing we'll do is try to locate Nate Bennett," said one of the officers. "If we can't find him, we'll put out an APB, that's All Points Bulletin. We'll have every officer in the city looking for him. As soon as we find him, we'll take him into custody. Kidnapping's a serious crime."

Sarah couldn't believe what she was

hearing. She couldn't believe that she was responsible for the arrest of anyone, let alone someone she'd known since grade school.

"Thank you for caring enough to come forward, Sarah," said Mr. Armstrong as they all stood up to leave.

"You're welcome, Mr. Armstrong," said Sarah. "I just hope they find Jenny soon."

* * *

By Monday morning, Nate Bennett had not been found. Neither had Jenny nor Coach Brown's baby. When Sarah got to school, she noticed the somber mood that hung over the building like a dark cloud. Everyone is affected by this, she realized.

"Sarah, did you hear the news?" Tina asked when Sarah got to history class. "The police questioned the nurses at the hospital where Mr. Brown's baby was born. Several of them said they saw someone who looked like Nate Bennett hanging around the newborns' nursery the day the baby was kidnapped. This is too weird. I can't believe we know someone who's involved in a kidnapping."

NEW KID IN CLASS

"Yeah, I just wish I'd have realized how dangerous he was before," Sarah said. "Maybe some of this wouldn't have happened."

Sarah saw James in biology class seventh period. He came to class late, and Mrs. Blakely had already started her lecture, so Sarah didn't have a chance to talk to him until after class.

"James," she said as they filed out of the classroom. "I'm so sorry about Jenny. You must be really upset."

"Yes, it's too bad," James said. "You just never know what's going to happen, do you?"

Sarah thought she had heard this conversation before.

"More than likely, the Armstrongs are never going to see Jenny again," James added. "I think the best thing they can do now is have a new child to get their minds off Jenny. Same thing with the Browns."

Sarah was shocked. It was practically the same thing he had said when Sadie disappeared. "James, how can you say such a thing? You're so cold, so insensitive. Do you have any idea how those people feel?"

"You Americans are too emotional," James said. "In my homeland, if parents lose an offspring, they simply produce another." With that, James walked away, leaving Sarah standing in the middle of the hall speechless.

Almost in a daze, Sarah headed toward the locker room. James' remark had really upset her. She couldn't believe anyone could be so unfeeling. Tina was certainly right. Something was not right about him. Nothing ever bothered him—not Nate Bennett, not the disappearance of a young girl or even a baby. Nothing. If that's the way he is, I'm glad he's not interested in me, she thought.

After changing her clothes, Sarah headed toward the track.

"Sarah!" someone hissed from behind her.

Sarah turned around to see Nate Bennett crouched in the bushes by the building. He was motioning for her to come nearer. Sarah was terrified by the sight of him. Was this it? she wondered. Was she next on his list?

Backing up, Sarah said, "No! Get away from me! I'll scream!"

"Sarah, please," Nate pleaded. "I won't hurt you. Just give me a chance!"

"Why should I believe you?" Sarah demanded. "You've hurt everyone you have a grudge against. How do I know I'm not next?"

"Sarah, I didn't hurt anyone," said Nate. "Honest. I know you think I did, but it's not true. I have to talk to you, just for a minute. I think I can explain about the disappearances."

Sarah hesitated.

"Please, Sarah," Nate said. "I don't have much time. The police are looking for me."

Sarah's old doubts returned. What if he didn't do it? At least give him a chance to explain, she thought to herself. Sarah moved slowly toward him but stopped a few feet away. He looked terrible. He had the hood of his jacket pulled up over his head, and his handsome, boy-like face was drawn with worry. His red eyes indicated he hadn't slept in days.

"So explain," she said.

"Sarah, the police came to my house Saturday morning," Nate began. "Luckily, my dad was too drunk to tell them where I was. As soon as I saw them, I climbed out my window and ran. I've been running ever since."

"Nate," Sarah said, "turn yourself in. It's the best way."

"No, Sarah, don't you see?" Nate asked. "I didn't do it—any of it. I know everyone thinks I did, but, honest, I didn't have anything to do with those disappearances."

"But if you didn't do it, why did you run from the police?" Sarah asked.

"I've been in trouble with the police before," said Nate. "Nothing too serious. But once they get your name, it seems like they suspect you of everything. I heard about Coach Brown's baby, and I figured they thought I had something to do with it. So I ran."

"But Nate, you made that threat to me," Sarah said. "You said we'd all pay for treating you bad."

"Threat?" Nate said blankly. "I didn't threaten you."

"Yes, you did, Nate. Last Wednesday

NEW KID IN CLASS 87

after track practice," Sarah said. "You were standing right here when you said it."

Nate shook his head. "I remember talking to you before practice, and I remember seeing James on the ground after Mr. Potter blew his dog whistle. But I left right after that. We had a social worker coming to our house. She was there the whole evening trying to get my dad to join Alcoholics Anonymous. You can check it out."

Sarah didn't believe him. "Then you dropped that dead mouse on me during seventh period on Friday. Don't deny that, Nate. I saw you."

"Dropped a dead mouse on you?" Nate cried. "Sarah, I was in detention all day Friday. Ask Mr. Reed. I didn't get out until the bell rang."

Sarah was confused. She'd seen Nate in the courtyard, she knew she had.

"But the nurses at the hospital," Sarah said. "They said they saw you on Friday, the day Mr. Brown's baby was stolen."

"No, Sarah, that couldn't have been me," Nate said. "I was still in detention, remember? It must have been someone who looked like me. I would never steal someone's baby."

Confused now more than ever, Sarah asked, "So what were you going to tell me about the disappearances?"

"I know you're going to think I'm crazy, Sarah," Nate said, "but I think James Olson had something to do with them."

"James?" cried Sarah. "Don't be ridiculous. He just moved here. Why would he want to—" Suddenly Sarah remembered James' reaction to the disappearances. He showed no emotion, no concern whatsoever. But that certainly didn't mean he'd had anything to do with the kidnappings.

"I don't know, Sarah," Nate was saying, shaking his head. "But I saw him hanging around Mr. Carlson's room the day the piranhas disappeared. I know that's not much to go on, but I think he might be mixed up in this. None of this stuff was happening until he came to Hawksville."

Sarah had to admit that Nate had a point. Still, she wondered, why would James do such a thing?

"But, Nate, why did you come here

tonight? What do you want from me?" Sarah asked.

"I came here to tell you to look out for him," Nate replied. "I can't explain it, Sarah, but there's something weird about him. He's different from us. And I don't mean just because he's not from our country. I've thought that since that night at track practice. He shouldn't have been able to hear that whistle, Sarah. No human can hear a dog whistle. It's not possible."

The dog whistle! Sarah still had it on.

"Oh, my gosh, I keep forgetting to return this to Mr. Potter," she said, pulling the end of the chain out of her jersey.

"Try it, Sarah," Nate said. "Blow on it as hard as you can. Go ahead."

Sarah put the whistle to her mouth and blew.

"Did you hear anything?" Nate asked. Sarah shook her head. "Neither did I," Nate said. "Not a thing."

Nate paused for a moment and then said, "I'm worried about you, Sarah. I've seen the way he looks at you. I don't want you to be next on his list."

That's odd, Sarah thought. I was worried about being next on your list. So who's the bad guy here, anyway? she wondered.

"Plus I had to explain," Nate continued. "I didn't want you to think I was a kidnapper. I could never stand it if you thought that."

Nate certainly sounded sincere, and once again, Sarah found herself feeling sorry for him. "I'll be careful, Nate," Sarah said. She heard Coach Brown blow the whistle to start practice.

"Look, Nate, I've got to go," said Sarah. "What will you do now? Where will you go?"

"I'd rather not tell you, Sarah," Nate replied. "That way, if the police question you, you won't have anything to tell them. But don't worry about me. I'll be fine. Good-bye, Sarah. And take care of yourself." With that, Nate pulled his hood up over his head and disappeared around the corner of the building.

Nate had taken a big risk coming to warn her. Sarah decided she owed it to him to check James out. And she knew just the guy who could help her—Alex.

Alex was late getting home that evening. Sarah didn't have a chance to approach him until after supper. When she did, she told him about her new suspicions.

"But I thought you said Nate Bennett did it," Alex said.

"I thought so," Sarah said. "But now I'm not so sure. I just have this funny feeling about James, and I need to find out if I'm right." She didn't tell him anything about seeing Nate that afternoon. "I thought maybe you'd help me."

"Sure, whatever I can do," Alex said.

"Great! Let's start by checking out where he lives," Sarah said. "He says he lives in the old warehouse district. It's awfully deserted down there—and it'd be pretty easy to get away with a crime."

"The old warehouse district?" Alex repeated. "How will we ever find him there?"

"I was depending on your expert detective skills," Sarah said.

"Thanks for the vote of confidence," Alex said. "But why the flattery?"

Sarah smiled. "I was hoping we could take your car."

"Let's go," Alex laughed, grabbing his keys.

As Sarah and Alex approached the warehouse district, Sarah noticed that the neighborhood had gone downhill fast. The deserted buildings looked like they hadn't had tenants in years. Most had broken windows. Others had little mounds of litter piled against them from the wind.

It was beginning to get dark. A few shabby-looking men sauntered down the street, scouting the sidewalks for unfinished cigarettes. Others just hung their heads and shuffled along. A few sat crumpled against the buildings, unmoving, as if they had nowhere to go, nothing to do.

"Look at those poor people," Sarah sighed. "I feel so sorry for them."

"Yeah," Alex said, "there are a lot of people out of work around here, that's for sure."

"Can you imagine a pair of scientists and their son actually living in this neighborhood?" Sarah asked.

"Doesn't sound right to me," Alex agreed. "See any sign of your friend from Jamaica?"

"Everything looks pretty deserted," Sarah said. "Wait! There's a light on in that old warehouse. See it?"

"Let's check it out," Alex said.

Alex parked in the alley next to the building, and he and Sarah got out of the car.

"Used to be a furniture warehouse," Alex observed as they approached the building. "Look, it's still got campaign posters from the Nixon/Humphrey election."

"Talk about ancient history," Sarah said. "We weren't even born when those guys were running!"

"Well, Sarah, up for taking a look inside?" Alex asked when they reached the entrance.

"Sure," Sarah said, feeling brave because her brother was with her. She was glad she hadn't tried to do this on her own.

The front door of the building stood ajar, and a mangy-looking cat slipped out as Alex and Sarah went in. They entered a large room filled with empty boxes and pallets. Sarah saw a stack of table legs in one corner. The end for this business must have come almost overnight, she thought.

"Imagine all the people who used to work here," Alex said.

"Yeah," Sarah said.

"Looking for me, Sarah?" A voice cut through the shadows. Sarah turned to see James Olson leaning against the doorway.

"Is this where you live, man?" Alex asked.

"Who are you?" James asked.

"James, this is my brother," Sarah explained. "Alex, this is James Olson."

"Two visitors!" James said in mock surprise. "Am I under investigation?"

"No, I was just curious about you, James," Sarah said. "It's hard for me to believe that you and your family live here in a deserted furniture warehouse."

"We live upstairs," James said. "Our apartment isn't fancy, but there's a skylight in the ceiling that provides a marvelous view of the heavens. Would you like to see it?"

Sarah looked at Alex, who nodded. "Why not?" she said, trying to sound casual.

The three of them got into the freight elevator and rode to the top floor. The old elevator wheezed and creaked as it crawled up the shaft. It shuddered when the doors finally opened. James led them down a dusty hallway and stopped outside a door with the number 425 painted on it.

"Home," James announced, opening the door. "It's not much but it's cozy."

Sarah looked around. The apartment was pretty bare. There was a fancy computer and a chair in one corner and some odd-looking containers in another. She could also see James' skates and his book bag, but that was about it. The odor of spice Sarah had constantly smelled on James filled the room. It seemed to be coming from the containers in the corner.

"Look!" James pointed at the skylight in the ceiling. By now it was dark outside. The black sky was cross-stitched with glowing constellations.

"There are a hundred billion stars in the galaxy," James said. "And billions of galaxies. Stunning, isn't it? Ah, it reminds me of home."

"Stars and galaxies remind you of home?" Sarah repeated.

"Oh…um…we can see the same constellations from Jamaica," James added quickly.

Sarah recognized several groups of stars from the astronomy course she'd taken one summer at the science museum. But then she noticed other bright lights she'd never seen before. It was as if new planets had moved into view.

"What are those bright lights?" she asked.

James winked at her and said, "Optical illusions—just like the scorpions."

Remembering the scorpions, Sarah suddenly felt uneasy, even with Alex beside her. "We have to go now, James," she said.

But Alex wasn't quite ready. He looked closely at James. "You're a runaway, aren't you?" he asked. "Your parents aren't living here. There's not a kitchen or anything. You're holed up here by yourself, right?"

"Is it any of your business?" James said calmly.

Sarah continued to stare at the bright lights above. They seemed to be drawing closer. They were the most brilliant lights she'd ever seen. "Please, Alex, I want to go now," she said, tugging at her brother's sleeve.

"Just a minute, Sarah," Alex said. "Look, James, I don't care if you're living here by yourself. You're right. It's none of my business. But a lot of strange things have happened since you came to Hawksville. I'd watch my step if I were you."

"I assume you're referring to the disappearances," said James. "If I remember correctly, they know who was responsible for them. Nate Bennett, remember?"

"Nothing's been proven against Nate, James," Sarah reminded him.

James smiled. "Oh, but it will be, I assure you, Sarah. After all, everyone's here for a purpose—even Nate Bennett."

"Come on, Sarah," Alex said, steering her toward the door. "Let's go."

Alex and Sarah left the apartment and hurried down the hall to the elevator. It seemed to take forever for the doors of the elevator to open. Once inside, Sarah pushed the button for the ground floor and leaned back in relief.

The elevator lumbered down its shaft, groaning as before. When it reached the ground floor, it landed with a thud. Sarah and Alex waited for the doors to open, but nothing happened.

"Any time now," Alex said. But the doors remained shut. He looked around for an emergency button, but there wasn't any. "So what now?" he grumbled. "Come on, doors! Open!"

Icy fear gripped Sarah. "Alex!" she cried. "James did this. I know he did. He must have a way of controlling the elevator from upstairs, and he made it stop. What are we going to do?"

"Now, don't panic," Alex said. "Could be this ancient elevator is just being temperamental. Let's give it another minute." But a minute later, Alex was shouting, "Come on, Olson, stop the games. Get these doors open!"

"We didn't tell anybody where we were going," Sarah groaned. "If we don't come home, Mom and Dad won't even know where we are!"

Sarah closed her eyes. She felt sick with terror. Maybe Nate had been right. Maybe James Olson was mixed up in the disappearances. And now she and Alex knew where he lived. They knew his secret haunt. Maybe he didn't want anybody to know. Maybe he would make them disappear like the others had.

"Smoke!" Alex said sharply. "I smell smoke, Sarah!" The fear in his voice made Sarah even more terrified. She fought the tears that came to her eyes.

"He…he set the building on fire!" she said, trying not to cry. "Don't you see, Alex? He's going to burn down the building with us in it because we've discovered his secret place. We're trapped here, and we're going to die!"

"Come on, Sarah, help me!" Alex ordered. He threw himself on the doors and tried to wedge his fingers in between them. Sarah did the same. But although they tried desperately to pry them open, the doors refused to budge.

"It's no use, Alex," Sarah said, falling back onto the floor. "They're stuck." She laid her head on her knees. "Oh, Alex, why did we ever come here?" she moaned.

8

SUDDENLY SARAH HEARD the doors slide open. She looked up to see James standing just outside. "This elevator," he said, shaking his head, "is so unpredictable."

"The building's on fire!" Alex cried, grabbing Sarah's hand for a mad dash from the building.

"No, no," James laughed. "Some transients have a fire going just outside the window. See them gathered around that barrel?" He pointed out the window. "Your nights certainly are chilly here."

"You stalled the elevator on purpose to scare us, didn't you?" Sarah asked bitterly.

James shook his head. "You're very suspicious, Sarah. You really should work on that."

Alex and Sarah hurried outside to where Alex's car was parked. "He's not going to get away with this," Sarah said.

Alex started the car and drove down the deserted street. "I hate to say this,

Sarah, but get away with what?" he asked.

"Alex!" Sarah cried, her heart sinking. "Don't tell me you don't believe me!"

"I didn't say that, Sarah, but look, maybe the old elevator really did get stuck. I mean, what are we going to say? That James tried to murder us because the elevator was stuck for two minutes?"

"But, Alex, he's lying about his parents living there. Anybody can see that," Sarah insisted. "And he told me he was the middle child. Well, I didn't see any signs of brothers or sisters around, did you?"

"Maybe the guy is on his own, but is that a crime?" Alex asked. "Should we turn into a bunch of busybodies just because he's a loner?"

"I'm telling you, he's strange, Alex," Sarah said. "I know now he had something to do with the disappearances! I can feel it. And I think he's trying to frame Nate Bennett."

"No, you don't know it, and that's the problem," Alex said. "I know the guy is weird, Sarah. I could tell that just by talking to him. But if weird were a crime, the jails would be even more full than they already are. Just stay away from him, okay? If he's hiding some deep, dark secret, it'll come out, and he'll get busted."

If they don't catch Nate Bennett and blame it on him first, Sarah thought. Poor Nate. I wonder where he is and how he's doing. I wish I could help him.

* * *

At school the next day, James was waiting for Sarah by her locker.

"Hello, Sarah," he said sweetly.

"Don't talk to me, James," Sarah said, opening her locker.

"But Sarah, what's wrong?" he asked with mock concern.

Sarah looked at him. She could tell by his eyes that he was laughing at her.

"Just leave me alone. I don't want anything to do with you," she said.

"You didn't feel that way a few days ago," James reminded her. "And last night you even brought your brother to meet me. Why, I feel like I'm almost part of the family. All I have left to meet now is your parents."

Sarah looked at him and narrowed her eyes. "What do you mean?"

"Nothing," James replied. "Only that I've met your younger sister—Melissa, I believe it is?"

"When did you meet Melissa?" Sarah demanded.

"Last week when she gave me your bracelet and a sample of your hair," James answered. "She's a charming little thing, isn't she?"

Sarah was confused. "But she said she gave those things to Nate Bennett. She described him."

"Oh, yes, she saw Nate Bennett, all right," James said. "But it was really me."

"I don't understand," Sarah said, confused.

"It's a talent I have," James smiled. "I'm quite capable of making myself look like others. It's a little thing we Jamaicans are quite good at."

"You mean you use makeup?" Sarah asked.

"Something like that," James said.

"But why did you want those things of mine?" Sarah wanted to know.

"As I told you before, Sarah, everything has its purpose," James said. "It's amazing what things one can learn from a little strand of hair!"

"What kinds of things?" Sarah asked, not sure that she wanted to know.

"Oh, I have ways of finding out your entire genetic makeup, Sarah," James said, "just by running tests on a piece of your hair. By the way, you come from very good stock. As does your little sister, of course."

"My sister! You leave her out of this!" Sarah cried.

"Oh, she's young now, but I think she has an excellent chance of becoming a perfect little specimen," James said.

Sarah glared at James. "Don't you call her a specimen! That's what you called Mr. Potter's dog before it disappeared! And Jenny! You leave my sister alone, do you hear?" She didn't notice that her loud voice was bringing stares from the students who were passing by.

"Don't be a hysterical fool," James said, looking around. "You're making a scene."

"I'm warning you, if anything happens to Melissa, I'll see that you're caught and punished!" Sarah said between clenched teeth.

"My, how your eyes flash when you get angry. That is so interesting. Little flecks of dancing fury," James said, enjoying Sarah's reaction.

Sarah reached up and slapped James across the face. She'd never done anything like that before in her life, but he terrified and maddened her so much that she couldn't help it. Now, shocked, Sarah drew back. She realized she'd left a scratch on James' cheek with her fingernail. A tiny ridge of skin appeared, and a drop of pink liquid bubbled to the surface. Luckily, the halls had almost cleared, so no one else saw.

James closed his eyes and seemed to be concentrating intensely. Sarah backed up. She was afraid he was gathering his rage and preparing to strike her back.

But then, as Sarah watched, the welt on James' cheek flattened out, the liquid evaporated, and the scratch itself vanished. It was like watching the healing process on fast forward. It had all occurred within about twenty seconds.

"There now," James said. "That's taken care of. Well, off to class, eh?" And with that he strode away.

Sarah was badly shaken as she walked to history. How could James' face have healed in twenty seconds? And why hadn't red blood come out of the wound? What was that pink liquid? No one bled like that—at least no one human.

When Sarah entered the classroom, she saw Tina sitting with a group of students. They were talking in excited tones.

Tina looked up and said, "Hey, Sarah, did you hear about the latest disappearance? Mrs. Blakely's iguana is gone!"

"Iggy? Someone stole Iggy?" Sarah gasped. Mrs. Blakely had a small collection of live animals, mostly snakes and lizards, but Iggy was her pride and joy. She loved the startled looks he brought to the faces of her students on the first day of class every semester.

"It gets worse, Sarah," Casey Johnson, another junior, said. "I was in the classroom when Mrs. Blakely discovered that the lizard was gone. James Olson was there working on some special project. I overheard him tell Mrs. Blakely that you probably did it because she wouldn't let you switch lab partners. And he said you'd probably try to blame him because he didn't want to date you."

"Sarah," Tina said, "I think you'd better go see Mrs. Blakely—quick!"

Sarah's stomach knotted in fear. What was James trying to pull now? She'd have to wait until second period when she had study hall to find out.

History class seemed to take forever. Sarah was dying to get to the biology lab to clear her name with Mrs. Blakely.

During second period, Sarah got a pass from the study hall supervisor and headed for the biology room. Sarah knew that second period was Mrs. Blakely's planning time.

Sarah found the older woman sitting at her desk grading papers. "Mrs. Blakely, I just heard about your iguana. I'm really sorry."

Mrs. Blakely looked up, her eyes narrowing with suspicion. "Sarah, I have reason to believe you may know something about Iggy's disappearance."

"James Olson told you I took the iguana, didn't he?" Sarah asked. "He wants to get me in trouble, Mrs. Blakely."

"Sarah, don't talk nonsense." Mrs. Blakely scoffed. "James Olson would never do such a thing."

"Mrs. Blakely, listen to me, please! James was calling Mr. Potter's collie a wonderful specimen right before the dog vanished. He was with Jenny when she disappeared, and I've heard him say Iggy was the finest specimen of a reptile he's ever seen!" Sarah knew she sounded defensive and guilty as her voice rushed desperately on, but she didn't know what else to do.

"Mrs. Blakely, I think James is collecting things...animals and people! I even think he's the one who took Mr. Brown's baby. Think about it, Mrs. Blakely. He's your lab assistant. He has a key. It would be so easy for him to steal Iggy."

"James has a key to the lab because I trust him completely," Mrs. Blakely snapped. "The person who took Iggy broke a window to get in!"

"But James is so clever, Mrs. Blakely, don't you see?" Sarah insisted. "He would have done that just to throw suspicion off himself."

"Sarah, apparently I misjudged you," Mrs. Blakely said. "I thought you had a level head on your shoulders. I never dreamed you'd let some silly romance gone sour lead you to foolish behavior. But it appears that you've allowed your feelings for James Olson to take you down a most unfortunate path."

"You've judged and convicted me on the word of James Olson!" Sarah cried. "That's so unfair!"

"Hardly, Sarah," Mrs. Blakely said. "I'm a scientist, remember? I need proof, hard proof, before I make a decision."

"Proof?" Sarah said. "I don't understand."

"When I found Iggy's cage broken into," Mrs. Blakely began, "I also found something else. The thief was so anxious to steal my iguana that she inadvertently dropped something that identified her. It was still on the floor right under the table that holds the cage."

Mrs. Blakely reached into her desk and held something aloft. It was Sarah's old

I.D. bracelet. "I suppose you will deny this is yours, but it bears your initials."

Sarah stared at the bracelet. "It is mine, but…"

Melissa's taunting words came back to her. "Remember that I.D. bracelet you threw away last week? Well, I dug it out of the trash and saved it. I gave him that too. You should have heard him. He was so-o-o-o happy, you would've thought I'd given him gold."

"My little sister gave that bracelet to James Olson," Sarah said. "He must have deliberately left it at the scene of the crime!"

"Oh, Sarah! Give it a rest!" Mrs. Blakely cried in exasperation. "Stop trying to lie your way out of this. Now listen to me and make no mistake—I mean business. Unless you return that animal within twenty-four hours, I'm going to report this to the police. Iggy is not only dear to me, but he's worth a lot of money. The theft of that lizard is a serious crime!"

"Mrs. Blakely, I know you don't believe me, but it's true," Sarah said. "I'll prove it to you. I'll have my mom bring Melissa here after school. She'll tell you what happened."

"I'll be here, Sarah," said Mrs. Blakely. "But, frankly, I think it would be easier if you simply returned my iguana."

Right before seventh period, Sarah called her mother and told her everything. Mom promised to pick up Melissa after school and bring her directly to Hawksville High to talk to Mrs. Blakely.

"Mom," Sarah said, "be sure to tell Melissa I'm really counting on her, okay?"

When Sarah hung up the phone, she saw James Olson standing there, arms folded. He had overheard most of the conversation.

"You're in the spider's web, Sarah," he warned. "The more you struggle, the more tangled you become."

"You stole the iguana and tried to frame me, James Olson," Sarah said. "Well, it won't work! My little sister will tell Mrs. Blakely who had the I.D. bracelet, and you'll—"

"Poor Sarah," James interrupted her. "I'm rather grateful not to be burdened with emotions because I think I should find your hopeless struggles too painful to endure."

"Mrs. Blakely will soon know the truth," Sarah said.

"If you say so, Sarah," James said. He offered her his arm. "Shall we go to biology now?"

Sarah thought to herself that she'd never both hated and feared anyone in her life until now. She hated James Olson with all her heart. She stomped into class ahead of him.

Sarah was glad they weren't having lab that day. Instead, Mrs. Blakely was lecturing. Sarah sat glumly next to James, not saying a word the entire hour. When the bell rang, she raced out to the parking lot, grateful when she saw the family car with her mother and Melissa in the front seat.

"Oh, am I glad to see you, Melissa," Sarah cried. "Come on. Mrs. Blakely is waiting."

The three entered the biology room, and Sarah introduced her mother and sister to Mrs. Blakely. Then she said, "Okay, Melissa. Remember that big iguana I showed you once?" Melissa nodded. "Well, it's disappeared, and Mrs. Blakely thinks I took it. She found my I.D. bracelet near the cage. Now, will you tell Mrs. Blakely what you did with my I.D. bracelet—who you gave it to?"

Melissa was obviously nervous. She squirmed under the stares of the others. "I don't know anything about your bracelet," she said.

"Melissa, yes you do!" Sarah said. "Remember the night you came home late—"

"You said you wouldn't tell. You promised!" Melissa started to cry.

Oh, no, Sarah thought. I did promise. But this is more important.

"Mom," Sarah pleaded, "will you tell Melissa she won't get in trouble? This is really important, Mom."

Mrs. Jackson put her hand on Melissa's shoulder. "Melissa, dear, listen. Your sister really needs your help here. Just tell the truth and don't worry about anything else."

Melissa stopped sniffling.

"Okay, Melissa," Sarah said. "Tell Mrs. Blakely what happened to my bracelet."

"I gave it to Nate Bennett," Melissa blurted out.

"Nate Bennett!" Mrs. Blakely exclaimed. "I might have known he had something to do with this. Is that who you're teaming up with nowadays, Sarah?"

"But Mrs. Blakely...," Sarah stammered. She'd forgotten that Melissa really did think it was Nate Bennett she had talked to. "It wasn't Nate Bennett. It was James Olson. James himself told me so. He only made himself look like Nate Bennett..." Sarah's voice faded off as she realized Mrs. Blakely didn't believe her.

"Melissa," Mrs. Blakely said, "tell us again to whom you gave the bracelet."

Melissa started to cry again. "I'm sorry, Sarah, but you said it was Nate Bennett when I described him to you," she said between sobs.

Sarah tried one more time. "But remember, Melissa? You said he smelled funny, like spice. Right?"

Melissa nodded her head.

"What does that prove?" Mrs. Blakely wanted to know.

"Mrs. Blakely," Sarah began, "haven't

you ever noticed that James Olson always wears some kind of spicy aftershave or cologne?"

"Yes, but, I still don't see..." Mrs. Blakely replied.

"Melissa said the person she gave my bracelet to smelled spicy, just like James Olson," Sarah said. "Don't you see, Mrs. Blakely, James makes himself look like other people. He made himself look like Nate Bennett when he talked to Melissa. And I think he did the same thing the day I fainted in biology. Someone threw a dead mouse on me right before I passed out. I thought it was Nate Bennett, but Nate was in detention that day."

"You never said anything about anyone throwing a dead mouse on you, Sarah, if I remember correctly," Mrs. Blakely said. "And how can you accuse James of such a thing? He's the one who helped you that day."

Sarah decided to give it one last shot. "Mrs. Blakely, the nurses said they saw a boy who looked like Nate Bennett at the hospital the day Mr. Brown's baby was stolen. But Nate was in detention that day.

He wouldn't have had time to get to the hospital and take the baby…"

Sarah could see that Mrs. Blakely didn't believe her, that she didn't want to believe her. The teacher had made up her mind that James Olson could do no wrong.

Mrs. Blakely shook her head. "Sarah, give it up," she said. "You're only making yourself appear more guilty. If I were you, I'd—"

Mrs. Jackson interrupted her. "Mrs. Blakely, I appreciate your concern over the loss of your iguana. I realize he was a very valuable animal. But I know my daughter, and she would never do such a thing. Nor would she lie about someone else's involvement in the disappearance."

"Then how do you explain the bracelet?" demanded the teacher.

"I don't know," Mrs. Jackson admitted. "But I do know that if Sarah says she had nothing to do with the theft, she had nothing to do with it. I suggest you investigate this matter further. Right now I'm taking my daughters home."

In the car, it was Sarah's turn to cry. "Oh, Mom, what am I going to do?" she sobbed. "Mrs. Blakely will probably have me arrested."

"Take it easy, sweetheart," Mrs. Jackson said. "We'll get this straightened out. Nobody in her right mind could believe a child of mine is a thief."

"Sarah, I'm sorry," Melissa said.

"It's all right, Melissa," Sarah said. "You were only telling what you thought was the truth."

"Do you have track practice tonight?" Sarah's mother wanted to know.

"No," Sarah replied. "Mr. Brown hasn't come back to school yet."

"Then let's get you home," Mrs. Jackson said.

That evening the phone rang about ten o'clock. Sarah answered it in her bedroom.

"Hello, Sarah," James Olson said.

"What do you want?" Sarah demanded.

"I know that Mrs. Blakely has threatened to call the police about the iguana," James said. "I didn't realize she would take it that far."

"And?" Sarah snapped.

"I don't want you to have to worry

about the whole thing anymore," James said

"Have you decided to admit taking the lizard?" Sarah asked.

"Oh no, of course not. That would serve me no purpose," James said. "But we can't have you getting in serious trouble over this either. Just don't worry about it anymore. Nobody is going to call the police or anything like that." Then he hung up.

That's odd, Sarah thought. What did James mean, don't worry about it anymore? Sarah was pretty certain that if she didn't produce Iggy within twenty-four hours, Mrs. Blakely *would* call the police. What was James going to do about that?

9

SARAH TURNED ON the news. The Channel 5 news team was doing a segment about the disappearances. Apparently there were more than Sarah had heard of, and they were happening throughout Hawksville. They mentioned Mr. Potter's dog, Mr. Carlson's piranhas, and the iguana. Then they showed photos of Coach Brown's newborn baby and Jenny Armstrong. Under the pictures were the dates they had disappeared. It broke Sarah's heart to see Jenny and the baby on the screen.

The reporter went on to mention a few more animals that been reported stolen. One person lost his pet boa constrictor, and another her prize parrot. Then the reporter ended the segment by telling about the latest disappearance. It had taken place at another school, Adams High, on the east side of town. The handsome face of a blond-haired senior named Michael Kelly appeared on the screen.

Michael was an honor student and a star athlete, the reporter explained. He had disappeared several days ago after running in a track meet. In interviews, his weeping parents and friends expressed disbelief. "How could such a talented and successful young man just walk away from everything?" they sobbed.

Michael's classmates were interviewed next, and then, suddenly, Sarah's eyes opened wide. A boy who looked just like James Olson appeared on camera. The reporter introduced him as Edward Jefferson from Jamaica! The boy said in a flat voice, "We all liked and respected Michael. He was a splendid specimen of an athlete."

Sarah gasped. A specimen! How many times had James used that word! James Olson and Edward Jefferson must be in this together, Sarah thought. But why were they stealing animals and people?

Sarah ran down the list of disappearances in her mind. What could James and the other boy possibly want with a dog, two piranhas, an iguana, a newborn baby, and a teenage boy and girl?

Sarah went to school the next morning feeling like she might be going to her own ruin. Mrs. Blakely's time limit for the return of Iggy was running out. But, as Sarah approached her locker, an excited Casey Johnson appeared. "Sarah, did you hear what happened to Mrs. Blakely?" he panted.

"What?" Sarah gasped.

"They think she's gone," Casey said. "Her car was in the teachers' parking lot all night. She never went home, and she's not here at school. I heard Mrs. Grant and Mr. Potter talking when I came in early for band practice."

"Oh, no!" Sarah groaned. This was what James had meant when he said Sarah shouldn't worry about Mrs. Blakely anymore!

Sarah glanced up and saw the Channel 5 news team entering the building. They had cameras and microphones and seemed to be in a hurry. Mrs. Grant greeted them solemnly and stood talking in low tones to the reporter. As Sarah and other students watched, the team set up their equipment in front of the trophy case.

Then the cameraman started his camera, and the reporter began speaking into her microphone.

"Good morning. This is Salli Harmon reporting to you live from Hawksville High, where there have been a number of unexplained disappearances lately. I'm standing here with Mrs. Grant, principal of Hawksville." She turned to Mrs. Grant. "Principal Grant, I understand that you've just become aware of yet another disappearance—that of Mrs. Constance Blakely, a biology teacher here at the school."

Sarah heard several students gasp around her.

"That's right," Mrs. Grant said. "We have reason to believe that Mrs. Blakely may have disappeared some time after the end of the school day yesterday."

"And I understand that police are looking for a student here at the school—a Nate Bennett, is that correct, Mrs. Grant?" the reporter asked.

"Yes, that's right," Mrs. Grant said.

"Can you speculate on Nate Bennett's motives, Principal Grant?" the reporter continued. "What might be the reason for

NEW KID IN CLASS

his alleged actions?"

"Well," Principal Grant began, "evidently Nate Bennett has had a grudge at one time or another against the people who were affected by these disappearances—the owners of the dog and the piranhas, the father of the baby who was stolen, the teenage girl herself, Jenny Armstrong."

"What about Mrs. Blakely?" Salli Harmon asked. "What kind of grudge did he have against her?"

"That we don't know yet," Mrs. Grant said. "The police are still looking into it."

"Thank you, Principal Grant," the reporter said. "And now we'd like to get reaction from some of the students here at Hawksville." She spotted Sarah in the crowd of students and moved toward her with the microphone. The cameraman followed.

"May I ask your name?" the reporter held the microphone close to Sarah.

"Sarah Jackson," Sarah said hesitantly. She'd never been on camera before.

"Sarah, how do you feel about the disappearances here at Hawksville High?" Salli Harmon asked.

Sarah took a deep breath. She realized that this was her chance to clear Nate Bennett and cast suspicion on James Olson. But would anyone believe her, or would she sound like a child with an overactive imagination? It was worth a try, she decided. She had nothing to lose, and Nate Bennett had everything to lose.

"I think the disappearances are tragic," Sarah began, "but I don't think Nate Bennett had anything to do with them."

"So you're saying the young man is being wrongly accused?" the reporter asked. Sarah heard a murmur go through the crowd.

"Yes," said Sarah.

"Do you have any idea who might be responsible for these disappearances, Sarah?" Salli Harmon asked.

Sarah nodded. "I think there's something among us, something foreign, even alien, that might be doing this."

The reporter looked amused. "Excuse me," she said, "but did I hear you correctly? You're blaming the disappearances on an alien force?"

Sarah could hear snickers from the

crowd, and she realized how crazy she must sound. She decided not to say that she thought James was an alien but simply indicate that he might be involved. "I just think the police should investigate this whole thing a little further," she said. "I don't think they should assume that Nate Bennett did it. They should look closer at any new students in the area—both at Hawksville and at Adams."

"Interesting theory, Sarah," Salli Harmon said. "And I'm sure the police will follow it up. Now, let's move on to another student."

As Sarah went from class to class that day, she noticed a lot of the students were laughing at her.

One girl raised her fingers behind her head like antennae and said, "I am an alien from the planet Zircon. Who will be next to disappear?"

A boy called out, "Hey, Sarah, I think I saw the mother ship parked outside the building. Should I call the police?"

Even Tina seemed embarrassed by the whole thing. "Sarah," she said at lunch, "everybody's razzing me about having a best friend who believes in UFOs."

"Sorry, Tina," Sarah sighed. How could she explain?

"When I said James Olson was weird, Sarah, I didn't mean weird like an alien," Tina said. "I just meant, you know, regular weird."

"Yeah," Sarah said bitterly, "everybody thinks I'm crazy. Let me ask you, Tina—how many people have to disappear before somebody realizes that something is really wrong? And now it's started happening on the other side of town. Don't you find that odd?"

"Yes, I do," Tina agreed, "but that doesn't mean there are aliens involved. We've got plenty of weirdos right here on earth who are capable of kidnapping—and one of them might be James Olson, for all I know. But we don't need to blame it on aliens."

"We don't need to blame it on Nate Bennett, either," snapped Sarah.

"Since when are you such a fan of Nate's?" Tina asked. "I thought you couldn't stand him."

"I'm not his fan," Sarah said. "I just think he's being framed for something he didn't do, and it's not right. And before it happens again, I'm going to do something about it."

Instead of going home after school that afternoon, Sarah biked to the warehouse district. She didn't know for sure what she was looking for. She only hoped to find something that might prove James Olson was behind the disappearances. If she could do that, she could clear Nate Bennett of any involvement.

Sarah parked her bike behind the old furniture warehouse where James lived. She glanced around. Piles of trash littered the area, and weeds grew everywhere. A young man with a scruffy beard slept against the next building. On the ground beside him lay a brown paper sack with the neck of a liquor bottle sticking out. As Sarah watched, a rat appeared and began investigating the sack. Sarah shivered. This is not going to be easy, she thought.

She made her way quietly through the alley, glancing up now and then at the windows in James' building. She half-expected to see James' face leering down at her, and the thought nearly made her turn back.

I've come this far, Sarah told herself. I can't give up now.

She had reached the place Alex had parked his car the other night. No sign of James—or anyone else, for that matter. Other than the wino she had just seen, the whole area seemed deserted.

Silently, Sarah approached the entrance to the building. Again, the door was ajar, and she slipped inside. She decided to take the steps instead of the elevator. She couldn't risk James hearing her if he were home.

Sarah found the door to the stairwell and started up the stairs. Halfway between the first and second floors, she heard footsteps on the stairs above her— and they were headed her way. James? A transient? She couldn't take any chances. She turned around and began making her way back down the steps.

Sarah considered exiting the stairwell on the first floor. But she was afraid that whoever was above her would do the same since the first floor led to the outside. Then she would take the risk of being seen. What should she do? Her heart pounded so loudly that she thought for certain it could be heard echoing in the concrete stairwell. She decided to head for the basement and hope that whoever was coming wouldn't decide to do the same.

The stairwell darkened as Sarah slipped down to the last step and around a corner of a wall. She stood silently and listened. The footsteps stopped on the landing. Sarah held her breath. Then they turned and headed toward the basement. She froze. If she remained motionless, whoever it was might not see her. It was pretty dark in the basement, and he probably wouldn't be looking for anyone.

Sarah decided to stay where she was. Not daring to breathe, she waited while the footsteps drew nearer. A few seconds later, someone stood within three feet of Sarah. She choked slightly as she stifled a scream. The figure turned, trying to make her out in the dimness.

"Sarah!" he said.

10

"NATE! WHAT ARE you doing here?" Sarah gasped in relief. "I thought you were James."

"I thought *you* were James," Nate said. "What are you doing here?"

"I'm not sure," Sarah answered. "I was looking for a clue, something that might tie James into the disappearances. Is this where you've been hiding out?"

"Yes," said Nate. "Nobody ever comes down here. And I thought I could keep an eye on James. I was looking for the same thing you were—a clue of some kind."

"Did you find anything?" Sarah asked.

"Boy, did I," Nate answered. "Sarah, you're never going to believe this. Come on."

Nate led the way down a dark, musty corridor. As Sarah followed, she looked around her. The rafters of the ceiling were covered with thick cobwebs, and the walls were wet with mildew. Here and there a skeleton of a rat lay on the floor. Sarah shivered, and she hurried to keep up with Nate.

"Almost there," Nate said, glancing back at her. "Pretty creepy place, huh?"

"I'll say," Sarah said.

Nate stopped at a door the led to the right. "Here we are," he said. "Sarah, I have to warn you, what you're going to see isn't pretty. But it's the proof we need that James is behind this. Are you ready?" Sarah nodded. Nate took her hand in his and gently squeezed it. He opened the door and led Sarah to the middle of the room, where he reached up and pulled the string to turn on the light.

Sarah looked around and caught her breath. She couldn't believe her eyes. Lining the walls were large, transparent cases. And in each case was a body—a silent, motionless body that seemed to be suspended in the air around it.

Sarah walked over to the first case. It held Mrs. Blakely. The older woman had her eyes closed as if she were sleeping— and yet not sleeping. More like she was simply temporarily unaware of what was going on and, at any minute, would open her eyes. Next Sarah saw Michael Kelly, the handsome senior from Adams High. His blond hair was arranged neatly on his head. He, too, had his eyes closed as though he were sleeping. Sarah turned to the next case. The body of Jenny Armstrong, beautiful Jenny, hovered weightlessly in midair. Sarah had the feeling that if the case were opened, Jenny would simply float away. Sarah knew what was next and hesitated, closing her eyes.

"It's all right, Sarah," said Nate, coming up behind her. "You don't have to look."

But Sarah opened her eyes and there, in a container not much bigger than a shoe box, was Coach Brown's baby boy. He was wrapped in a light blue blanket and had a little knit stocking cap on. Unlike the others, he seemed to be sleeping deeply, his tiny fingers clutching the blanket.

Sarah looked around the room. In other cases of assorted sizes were the animals that had disappeared—Mr. Potter's beautiful dog, Sadie, the piranhas, and Iggy, Mrs.

Blakely's prize iguana. Other animals were in cases nearby. Gazing around, Sarah saw a parrot, a rabbit, a boa constrictor, and a batch of kittens.

There were more cases on the other side of the room with people Sarah didn't recognize. One case held a man who appeared to be about forty. He wore the uniform of a police officer, and his badge read "Freeman." In the case next to him, was a little girl in a green and white soccer uniform. Sarah thought she looked about five years old. And nearby was a very old man and next to him, a very old woman. Sarah wondered if they were married.

Sarah began to cry softly. What had James done to these people and to these animals? And why?

She approached the last case in the room. Tears blurred her vision, and she looked down and wiped them away with the back of her hand. As her vision cleared, she noticed that the person in the case had on in-line skates. She looked up and saw a girl about ten years old. Sarah felt her knees go weak. Her pulse pounded in her ears, more loudly than before, and her breath came in short, hard gasps.

She covered her mouth with her hands and screamed, "Melissa! Oh, Nate, he got Melissa! Help me, Nate! Help me get her out of here!"

Sarah groped at the case. She hit it with her fists and kicked it with her feet. But it was no use. The sides were made of a synthetic material, and it would take more than human hands and feet to break it.

Nate was beside her immediately. He grabbed her by the shoulders. "Sarah, don't," he said. "It won't do any good."

Sobbing, Sarah fell against him. "Don't cry, Sarah," Nate said soothingly. "We'll get her out of here somehow."

"Oh, Nate, how could James have done this? Why did he do this?" Sarah whimpered.

"I don't know," Nate answered, putting his arms around her. "I just don't know."

Sarah buried her face in Nate's shirt and cried some more. She couldn't help it. It was all too sad. So many wonderful people taken—snatched by James and imprisoned in cases as if they were on display. And her little sister was one of them!

Suddenly Sarah noticed a familiar odor—the spicy smell of James Olson's cologne. She drew back. "Nate!" she began, looking around frantically. "I think James…" But she stopped in mid-sentence, too shocked to continue. She was no longer looking at Nate Bennett. In front of her stood James Olson, his golden–brown eyes staring down at Sarah, his perfect white teeth gleaming in a false smile.

"James!" Sarah gasped.

"Hello, Sarah," said James smoothly. "Glad you came today. It saved me the trouble of locating you. I was going out to do just that when I heard you on the steps."

"How did you—?" Sarah stammered.

"Change?" James asked. "Oh, that's nothing. I come from a race of shape-shifters."

"Shape-shifters?" Sarah repeated. "I don't understand."

"I wouldn't expect you to understand, Sarah, although you will soon enough," James said. "You've obviously figured out that I'm not from Jamaica. Actually, I'm from a planet in the fifth galaxy, light years away from Earth. I doubt you've ever heard of it."

Sarah couldn't believe what he was saying. And yet, it all added up. "Why are you here?" she asked.

James said. "I told you, I'm a hunter. I travel the universe collecting specimens to study." He nodded at the cases. "This has been quite a successful expedition. These are the specimens we're taking with us from Earth."

"We?" Sarah repeated.

"Oh, there are several of us in your fine city of Hawksville," James explained. "That's how these other specimens got here. The other hunters in our expedition collected them."

Sarah remembered the news report. "Edward Jefferson, is he one of your hunters?" she asked.

"Of course," James said. "In fact, he'll be here soon. You remember the bright lights you saw in my sky light? That was actually our mother ship hovering nearby. She's coming tonight to transport us home—

after we've loaded our cargo, that is."

"But you can't take them with you! You kidnapped them!" Sarah cried.

"I suppose that's your term for it," James said. He reached into his pocket and pulled out a small canister about the size of an aspirin bottle. "Actually, all I did was expose them to this. It's a gas similar to the ether used in your hospitals. I simply hold it directly under the specimen's nose, and I've got them."

The spicy odor Sarah had smelled grew a little stronger. "That's the spicy smell!" she said.

"Yes, I carry some with me all the time. The gas actually has quite an unpleasant odor," James explained. "I managed to mask it with a common smell from Earth—cooking spices. Quite clever, don't you agree?"

"But what does the gas do to them?" Sarah asked.

"Oh, it simply makes them unconscious for awhile," James said. "Long enough for me to get them back here and prepare them for suspended animation." He nodded at the cases.

"Suspended animation?" Sarah asked.

"Yes, it slows down their vital body functions—breathing, for example," James explained. "It's the only way they could survive the trip to our planet. Then, when we're ready to begin our studies, we simply open the case and provide them with a high concentration of oxygen. They come around quite quickly and are fine—as if nothing ever happened."

"But there are so many," Sarah said, looking around the room. "How did you and the others manage to get away with stealing all of these people? And animals? Weren't any of you ever caught?"

"Oh, we all had our Nate Bennetts," James said. "And they all served their purpose very well."

"You said you collect specimens for study," Sarah said. "What do you do with them when you're done studying them?"

"We put the more interesting ones in our zoos," James said. "We are quite well-known throughout our solar system for our zoos, actually." Then he shrugged. "The others we simply…dispose of."

"Zoos? Dispose of?" Sarah cried.

"James, you can't do this. These people have families. These animals belong to people who care about them. Don't you see how wrong this is?"

"It may be considered wrong on your planet, Sarah, but, on mine, it's perfectly acceptable—even expected," James said smugly. "But you'll find that out soon enough."

"What do you mean?" Sarah asked, afraid of the answer.

"You're coming with me," James said. "You didn't think I'd let a perfect little specimen like you get away, did you?"

"No, James, please" Sarah pleaded, backing away from him.

"Sarah," James said as he followed. "You can't get away from me. Besides, you might like my planet. When I described it to you earlier, you said you'd love to visit it."

"That was when I thought you lived in Jamaica!" Sarah cried.

"Come, come, Sarah, we've no time to lose. Our ship is returning to pick us up shortly." He moved closer.

This is crazy, Sarah thought. Crazy and terrifying. I can't believe it's happening.

She glanced around the room. At the top of one of the walls was a small window. The only other way out was the door.

"Sarah!"

Sarah and James looked at each other as footsteps pounded down the hall. Before Sarah could answer, Nate Bennett came flying through the doorway.

"Sarah! I'm so glad I found you! I saw your bike outside. Are you all right?" Nate asked, breathlessly. Then he spotted James Olson, and his eyes narrowed in distrust. "Leave her alone, Olson," Nate warned. "Sarah's not going into one of your boxes."

"Nate, you knew about this?" Sarah asked.

"Yes, I discovered it earlier today," Nate said. "I've been hiding out in the warehouse district, waiting for our friend here to make a mistake. I stumbled into this while he was in school."

"My, aren't you clever?" James said, smiling. "Oh, well, one more is better than one less. You might as well accompany Sarah on her little voyage. You'll be easy enough to dispose of once we're through with you."

"I'm not going anywhere with you, Olson," Nate said. "And neither is Sarah."

James opened the canister, held it at arm's length, and waved it through the air. Sarah could smell the odor of spice beginning to fill the room.

"Nate! That's some kind of ether!" Sarah cried, covering her nose and mouth. "Look out!"

Nate grabbed her hand. "Let's get out of here!" he yelled.

But when Sarah turned to run, she couldn't believe her eyes. Standing in the doorway was James Olson, actually five James Olsons. Exact replicas. Tall, slender young men with velvet brown skin, high cheekbones, and eyes that glowed like golden-brown gems. And they were coming into the room toward Sarah and Nate.

Sarah looked at Nate helplessly. The spicy odor was growing stronger. They were trapped. There was no way out.

Suddenly Nate said, "Sarah! Do you still have the whistle?" Sarah looked at him blankly. "The dog whistle!" Nate said. "Potter's dog whistle!"

Sarah reached into her shirt and pulled. The whistle still hung at the end of her chain.

"Blow it! Now!" Nate cried.

Sarah put the whistle to her lips and blew with all her might while Nate ran to open the window. As if struck by a bolt of lightning, James dropped to the floor in front of them. He covered his ears with his hands and moaned, "My ears! My ears!"

Sarah turned around. The other James Olsons were doing the same. As Sarah blew, she heard sirens outside the building.

"The police!" Nate said. "I called them right before I came."

Soon footsteps were pounding down the hall. Several police officers burst through the doorway.

"What in the—" said one officer, looking at the writhing bodies on the floor.

"Holy cow!" said another, spotting the cases.

Sarah choked. She couldn't blow the whistle anymore. She had run out of breath. She tore it off her neck and threw it to Nate, who put it to his lips but then stopped. He was staring at the group of bodies on the floor. Sarah looked down and couldn't believe what she saw. The aliens were changing. Their features were becoming blurry, and they were shrinking. Their arms and legs seemed to melt away, and as they continued to shrink, their bodies became bird-like. Suddenly Sarah was looking at a flock of tiny, shimmering purple birds. As she watched in astonishment, the flock disappeared out the window.

Suddenly from outside, a blinding light filled the basement room. For a few seconds, Sarah heard a soft humming sound, and then all was silent.

"They're gone," she said softly. Nate nodded. Then the room was silent, as if everyone there was too shocked to speak.

Finally one of the officers asked, "What just happened here? And why are those people in those cases?"

"We'll explain later," Nate said. "Sarah, did James tell you how to get these people out of the cases?"

"He didn't say how the cases opened," Sarah answered, "but he did say to give them a high concentration of oxygen to bring them out of suspended animation."

"Let's move," one of the policemen said. Several officers set about trying to figure out how to open the cases. Another went to the squad car to call for paramedics and oxygen tanks.

"Are you okay, Sarah?" Nate asked, as he and Sarah sat down on the floor to wait.

Sarah nodded. "Yeah. How about you?"

"I'm fine. A little hungry, though," Nate answered. "I haven't eaten much lately."

"You want to get a pizza when this is all over with?" Sarah asked, smiling.

"Is that a date?" Nate asked.

Sarah laughed. "Yeah, I guess it is."

"I see you've finally come to your senses," Nate said.

Sarah laughed again and then added quietly, "I'm sorry I misjudged you, Nate."

"That's all right, Sarah," Nate said. "You had every right to misjudge me. I haven't exactly been a model of good behavior."

Sarah thought of Nate's home situation. "But you've had some bad breaks too."

"Yeah, but all that's going to change

now," Nate said. "I made up my mind while I was in hiding that I would try to patch things up at home. I'm going to see if I can talk Dad into going to AA."

"Good for you, Nate," Sarah said. "Do you think he'll agree to it?"

"I don't know," said Nate. "He drinks because he's in pain. And he's in pain because my mom left us. I can't bring her back, but maybe I can convince him to get on with his life. Maybe getting him to AA will help."

"I hope so, Nate," Sarah said. "I really do." She was quiet for a moment, then nodded at the cases and asked, "Nate, do you think they'll be okay?" Her voice cracked as she spoke.

Nate sighed and covered her hand with his. "I don't know, Sarah," he said. "I hope so. But we aren't going anywhere 'til we find out."

By the time the paramedics arrived, the officers had figured out how to open the cases. The first one they opened was Melissa's. Sarah and Nate waited anxiously as the paramedics placed an oxygen mask over Melissa's mouth and nose and opened the valve on the tank. Sarah could hear the hissing of the gas as it flowed through the tubes and Melissa's faint breathing.

"Give her a few seconds," one of the paramedics said, noticing Sarah's concern.

Sarah waited for what seemed like an eternity. Suddenly, the sound of Melissa's breathing grew louder, and a few seconds later, the ten-year-old opened her eyes.

"Melissa!" Sarah cried, grabbing her sister's hand. "You're all right!"

"Sarah?" Melissa said. "What happened? The last thing I remember is that boy..." Suddenly Melissa's eyes grew wide. She had spotted Nate Bennett's face in the crowd. "Sarah, get him away from me!" she cried. "That's the boy who..."

"It's all right, Melissa," Sarah said, squeezing Melissa's hand. "That's not him. That's not the boy who hurt you. Believe me. We'll explain later."

"Good," said one of the policemen. "Then explain the whole thing to us too, will you?" He turned to the paramedics and said, "While you check her out, we'll move on to the next case."

"Gotcha," one the paramedics answered, rolling up Melissa's sleeve. "Let's get your blood pressure, young lady."

Melissa checked out fine. And one by one the cases were opened and the "specimens" set free. Phone calls were made to families and to owners of the animals that had been reported stolen. It was dark by the time the first family showed up. But soon the streets of the warehouse district were alive with celebration as loved ones rejoined their families and people got their pets back.

"This is great, isn't it?" Sarah said to Nate and Melissa. "All these people back together with their families? Look! There's Mr. and Mrs. Potter. They've got Sadie back."

The Potters came over with their beloved collie. "Sarah and Nate," Mrs. Potter said, "we just can't thank you enough."

"That's all right, Mrs. Potter. We were glad to help," said Sarah.

"And young man," Mr. Potter said to Nate, "I think I've been a little hard on you lately. Why don't you come into my office tomorrow morning, and we'll talk. Let's work on keeping you in class instead of out of it. What do you say?"

"Great, Mr. Potter," Nate replied. "I'll be there."

"Oh, Mr. Potter," Sarah said. "I've got something for you." She turned to Nate, who handed her the dog whistle. "Here's your whistle back."

"Why, thank you, Sarah," Mr. Potter said. "I wondered where I'd lost that."

"You're going to need it now that you've got Sadie back," Sarah said.

"You sure you don't want to keep it?" Mr. Potter asked. "I've got another one at home."

"No, thanks," Sarah said, glancing skyward. The stars were bright against the night sky, and Sarah thought she could see a few unusually brilliant ones moving steadily away from them. "I don't think I'm going to need it again. But if I do, I'll let you know."

Nate took Sarah's hand in his. "You ready for that pizza now?" he asked. "The police said we could talk to them about all this tomorrow."

"Sure, I'm starving," Sarah said. She looked at Melissa. "I suppose you want to come?" she teased.

Melissa's eyes lit up. "Can I?"

"You bet," said Nate. "How could a guy pass up going out for pizza with two *perfect specimens* like you?"